DINGO CREEK CHALLENGE

Books by Robert Elmer

ADVENTURES DOWN UNDER

#1 / *Escape to Murray River*
#2 / *Captive at Kangaroo Springs*
#3 / *Rescue at Boomerang Bend*
#4 / *Dingo Creek Challenge*
#5 / *Race to Wallaby Bay*

THE YOUNG UNDERGROUND

#1 / *A Way Through the Sea*
#2 / *Beyond the River*
#3 / *Into the Flames*
#4 / *Far From the Storm*
#5 / *Chasing the Wind*
#6 / *A Light in the Castle*
#7 / *Follow the Star*
#8 / *Touch the Sky*

ROBERT ELMER

DINGO CREEK CHALLENGE

BETHANY HOUSE PUBLISHERS
MINNEAPOLIS, MINNESOTA 55438

Dingo Creek Challenge
Copyright © 1998
Robert Elmer

Cover illustration by Chris Ellison
Cover design by Peter Glöege

Published by Bethany House Publishers
A Ministry of Bethany Fellowship International
11300 Hampshire Avenue South
Minneapolis, Minnesota 55438

Printed in the United States of America by
Bethany Press International, Minneapolis, Minnesota 55438

Library of Congress Cataloging-in-Publication Data

Elmer, Robert.
    Dingo Creek challenge / by Robert Elmer.
    p.   cm. — (Adventures down under ; 4)
    Summary: In late nineteenth-century Australia, as tension mounts between the white settlers and a band of aborigines at Dingo Creek, thirteen-year-old Patrick takes sides when he helps teach the aborigines how to play cricket.
    ISBN 1–55661–926-X (pbk.)
    [1. Australia—Fiction. 2. Australian aborigines—Fiction. 3. Cricket—Fiction.] I. Title. II. Series: Elmer, Robert. Adventures down under ; 4.
PZ7.E4794Di   1998
[Fic]—dc21   97–45447
                                                                                  CIP
                                                                                   AC

To Scott and Zenita
—faithful!—
and of course Micah,
Corinna, and Justin.

MEET ROBERT ELMER

ROBERT ELMER is the author of THE YOUNG UNDERGROUND series, as well as many magazine and newspaper articles. He lives with his wife, Ronda, and their three children, Kai, Danica, and Stefan (and their dog, Freckles), in a Washington State farming community just a bike ride away from the Canadian border.

CONTENTS

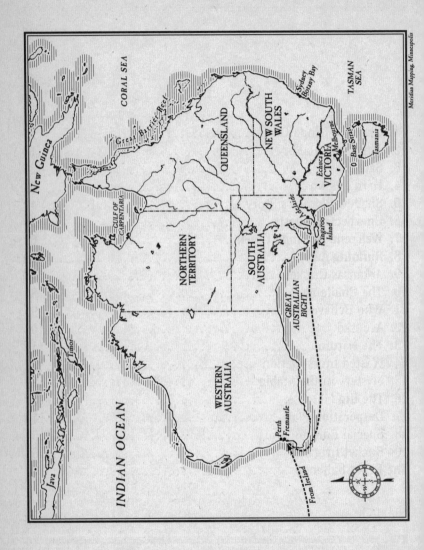

CORAL SEA

New Guinea

Great Barrier Reef

GULF OF
CARPENTARIA

QUEENSLAND

NEW SOUTH
WALES

Sydney
Botany Bay

TASMAN
SEA

NORTHERN
TERRITORY

SOUTH
AUSTRALIA

Adelaide

Echuca
VICTORIA
Melbourne

Bass Strait

Tasmania

Java

Timor

INDIAN OCEAN

WESTERN
AUSTRALIA

Kangaroo
Island

GREAT
AUSTRALIAN
BIGHT

Perth
Fremantle

From Ireland

N
W   E
S

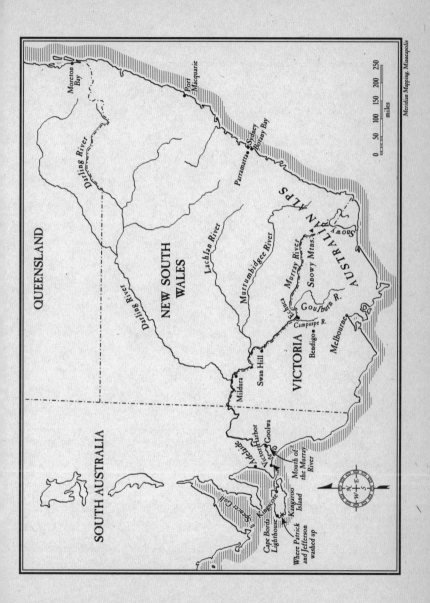

QUEENSLAND

NEW SOUTH
WALES

Darling River

Darling River

Lachlan River

Murrumbidgee River

Morton
Bay

Port
Macquarie

Parramatta ● Sydney
Botany Bay

AUSTRALIAN ALPS

Snowy Mtns.

Murray River

Echuca

Goulburn R.

Snowy Mtns.

Campaspe R.

Bendigo ●

Melbourne

Swan Hill

VICTORIA

Mildura

SOUTH AUSTRALIA

Adelaide ●

Victor Harbor ● Goolwa

Mouth of
the Murray
River

Spencer Gulf

Kingscote

Kangaroo
Island

Cape Borda
Lighthouse

Where Patrick
and Jefferson
washed up

Meridian Mapping, Minneapolis

miles

0   50   100   150   200   250

CHAPTER 1

CHAOS AT DINGO CREEK

"Why am I doing this?" thirteen-year-old Patrick McWaid asked himself as he threaded his way through a stand of eucalyptus trees toward the strange sounds up ahead. He stopped to look back at a low, red sun sinking behind clouds over the distant Murray River. Soon it would be dark. He was already too far away to see his grandfather's cabin on the other side of the river. But he still had time before dinner, if he hurried. . . .

He heard the sounds again, a faint clicking rhythm, a song that started softly and grew louder and louder. It was almost like a choir humming—a choir unlike any he'd heard.

"Strange." He scratched his red hair and listened again for the odd music drifting through the eucalyptus woods that hugged the Murray, close to the place called Dingo Creek. The almost beautiful wail came louder and higher, like a steamboat passing on the river, then softer and lower, like a bullfrog defending his *billabong*, or river backwater. On that evening in late August 1868, the damp, heavy air seemed to carry the strange rhythm and the song, making it hard to tell how far away it really was.

When they had both been back at the cabin a half hour earlier, his sister, Becky, had told him it was just a strange animal of some kind. A cricket, maybe.

Easy for her to say, Patrick thought to himself. *Everything here in Australia is strange compared to back home in Ireland.*

But she was right. After all, there *were* plenty of odd Australian creatures they didn't even know about yet. And since she hadn't wanted to come see for herself, Patrick would find out alone.

At fifteen, Becky was two years older than Patrick, but much smaller than her brother, petite and pretty like their mother.

Probably smarter, too, he told himself. *At least smarter for not wandering out here alone.*

Patrick, on the other hand, thought that he looked more like his father, except for his freckles, the way his big hands and feet didn't quite go with the rest of his body, and his fiery Irish green eyes. Then there were his ears, which tended to stick straight out from his head and were now tuned to the sounds up ahead.

"That's no animal," he had told her before slipping out the door. "It's more like music, I think."

"Hmm." She had not been convinced. "Tell me what you find out." And just like that she had returned to the shirt she was mending.

Maybe it *was* music, though surely it wasn't like any music Patrick had ever heard before back home in Dublin, Ireland. He remembered how bouncy fiddle music seemed to dance its way out open windows, through the Dublin streets, and into Patrick's ears. And the times at home after dinner when Patrick's father would carefully pull a tin whistle from its place on the shelf and play Irish tunes. More than once his mother had lifted her apron and skipped around the room.

But those had been happier times, before his father had been suddenly arrested for a crime he'd never committed and dragged to Australia on a dark prison ship.

Never mind that Patrick and the rest of his family had been able to follow, or that his father's name had been cleared, or that they had discovered in Australia the grandfather they'd never known. A paddle-steamer captain, yet. And tonight everything from the croaking frogs by the river to the strange music in the distance reminded Patrick that he was still a long way from Dublin—the only place he had ever called home. Patrick's thoughts snapped back to the present when he heard the bush chorus again.

He had to admit there was definitely a musical flavor to the weird sounds as he picked his way around the huge eucalyptus trees that looked even scarier in the shadows. In the dim light the bark of the trees looked like peeling paint. And up ahead he could just make out dancing shadows stretching themselves in front of a campfire.

Has to be aborigines, Patrick told himself as the beating of sticks and the singing became clearer and louder. He tiptoed closer, trying not to make any sound on the damp bed of flat eucalyptus leaves.

Patrick's grandfather had once told him about how the first Australians gathered to tell their stories through music and dances. "Corr-o-bor-EEs," he had called them. But by that time, 1868, there weren't very many aborigines left along the Murray River. Patrick hadn't heard why they had left or where they had gone, but he saw very few in Echuca, the river port town not far from his family's cabin. This would be the first time he had seen more than one or two at a time, and he crept closer, like a moth drawn to a flame.

"Must be fifty of them," he whispered to himself.

Acting as if they had no audience, a dozen dark aborigine women sat cross-legged in the dirt on one side of the clearing and served as an orchestra. Some beat two sticks together to keep time, while others beat on animal skins stretched across a crude frame. It hadn't seemed possible, but those were the strange noises he and Becky had heard from their cabin. The women hummed in low tones, sounding like a distant waterfall. A few children joined the act by beating their own sticks; one boy reminded Patrick of his younger brother, Michael, when he had been still younger.

Michael had had a toy drum when they lived in Dublin, over half a year ago now. Like most everything else, they had been forced to leave the toy behind. And it didn't seem to bother his brother as much as it had Patrick.

Michael's drum sure never sounded like this, Patrick decided after listening for a few more minutes. As he listened, the odd beat and singing sound drew him closer and closer, until Patrick was sure the dancing aborigines would see him staring at them.

Just a little closer, he thought, and sure enough, one of the aborigines finally noticed him. As Patrick stared like a captured animal, the dark woman—probably about his mother's age—nudged the woman sitting beside her and pointed in his direction. He quickly drew back into the shadows.

But the action didn't stop. Ten aborigine men gathered on the "stage" in the middle of the clearing. Each man was decorated on his chest and face with ghostly pale clay paint. Some crouched in the dirt, while others seemed to act out the part of hunters with blunt-tipped sticks.

Almost like an opera. Patrick realized after a while that he was watching a kind of drama. Then a song leader—an old, wrinkled man with a tangled silver beard—stood in front of the musicians, swaying and clapping two sticks together. Patrick smiled as the actors moved in time to the music, sometimes forming a line, sometimes doing a fancy foot dance. Patrick lost track of time as he watched the dance and the story of the hunt.

The group with the pretend spears was painted with designs of triangles and stripes around their ankles, wrists, and faces, while the rest of their dark skin was gleaming. They wore very little else besides their white ceremonial paint—only a rough, loose-fitting cloth, like a towel, wrapped around their waists. As the actor-hunters circled the actor-animals, the music continued, but softer.

"Hmm!" said one of the aborigines, as if he approved, and they began to join their voices in an almost musical chant that sounded to Patrick something like *"Ah barra bandy dura, birin gorah."* They continued their song as the hunters circled their unsuspecting animals. Maybe the animals were supposed to be sheep; Patrick couldn't quite tell.

"Ah barra bandy dura, birin gorah!"

As they repeated it, the song slowly grew louder, faster, more intense. Patrick held his breath to see what would happen next.

Without warning the hunters pounced on the herd of actor-animals, blunt spears flying. The people cheered and Patrick jumped back in surprise. A couple of the animal actors scrambled up and ran away into the trees, but most were ceremonially tackled in the middle of the clearing, to the loudest of cheers.

"Ah barra bandy dura, ah!" shouted the audience once more. By that time the skin drums were deafening, the sticks were rattling, and the shouts became whistles and cheers while the hunters smiled proudly at their audience. Strangely caught up in the performance, Patrick wanted to clap, too, but he didn't dare step out of the shadows. And when the silver-haired master of ceremonies put his hands up, the shouts and screams instantly came to a halt. The people beating sticks and drums stopped. Even the women swaying in time to the music froze. When a shadowy figure stepped into the light on the far side of the clearing, Patrick's heart stopped, too.

"Don't let me interrupt anything," boomed a tall and very English-sounding fellow. He was about eighteen years old, and with his ragged red jacket and black cap, he looked as if he were on a fox hunt. But he held a flat, wicked-looking club at his side. And by the way he stepped up to the party, uninvited, he made it clear that he wanted very much to interrupt. Three or four more dark figures stood behind the hunter. None of them was aborigine.

CHAPTER 2

AFTER DARK RAID

Patrick stared at the white people who had barged into the celebration. Patrick thought he recognized a few of the others from Echuca, and one in particular.

"It's *him*," whispered Patrick.

One of the boys sneered with a slightly cross-eyed glare down a long hook nose, his top lip peeling back to display a set of wildly crooked teeth that seemed to point in every direction at once. Unfortunately, there was no mistaking who they belonged to. Sebastian Weatherby.

For a moment Sebastian looked straight at Patrick and opened his mouth as if to speak. But Patrick didn't wait; he ducked back into the shadows. Still hidden, Patrick slowly backed away from the scene, not eager to be anywhere near the big, meaty fist that had given him a black eye the first day at his new school in Echuca a couple of months back.

"I said, don't let us interrupt." The tall blond leader waved his hand in circles as if to urge them on. And when he moved to the side, Patrick could just make out an older white woman standing behind them. Looking horribly out of place, she pulled a thin white sweater up around her shoulders and shifted from foot to foot without looking up.

In the camp several of the aborigine men still had their hands on their spears, although Patrick knew they were only sticks for the dance, and not at all sharp. When a young boy stepped up to the silver-haired aborigine leader and whispered in his ear, he spoke calmly to his people, and they lowered their sticks.

"If you've come to watch," said the older man, "you may sit quietly at the edge of the clearing."

The aborigine man's English was clear and unmistakable. Patrick could see that he stared strangely in the wrong direction, though. And with every move of Sebastian and his gang, the young aborigine boy whispered into the man's ear. Patrick guessed the boy couldn't have been more than about four or five years old.

The man's blind, guessed Patrick. The careful movements of the silver-haired man told Patrick he had guessed right.

Unafraid, the intruder and his friends stepped boldly forward into the light of the fire. Patrick still hung back.

"Watch?" The gang leader laughed again and spat on the ground in front of him as he responded to the old man's offer. A couple of aborigine boys scrambled out of his way. "No, I came with my friends because I have a complaint."

"Tell him, Will," said Sebastian, grinning smugly.

Patrick didn't dare breathe; no one else in the aborigine camp made a move, either. Even the mangy, snarling dogs on the fringes of the camp stayed where they were.

"My aunt's horses have been stolen," announced the leader of the gang, the one named Will. "She saw you people run off with them, didn't you, Aunt Ruth?"

The woman nodded nervously but kept silent, and Will whispered a few words to her. She nodded again, then Will pointed at a cluster of young aborigine men standing near the fire.

"Those two, right there by the fire." Will sounded like a judge at a hanging trial. "Soon as the constable makes it, we're here to bring those two thieves in."

Most of the aborigines waited for their leader to translate, and the protests were plain when he did. Even in a strange language, Patrick could understand what must have been "We did no such thing!"

"You see no horses here, do you?" asked the old aborigine man, raising his voice above the murmurs of his people. "No one here would do anything like that."

"No, you wouldn't hide them here," answered Will. "But we'll find out where they are soon enough."

Almost as if he were an actor making his entrance in a play, a uniformed man on a big black horse glided noiselessly into the camp. He pulled the reins and halted his horse next to Will and his aunt. The badge on his chest glimmered in the light of the camp-fire, and he frowned under a wide, waxed mustache—the tips of which nearly made it to his ears, they were so long. Behind him came another man in the same uniform.

Will laughed and nodded up at the constable. "I think we found the ones we're looking for, Constable Fitzgerald."

Constable Alexander Fitzgerald made no move to get down from his saddle.

"Mrs. Wilson?" he asked, his eyebrows raised. "You're quite certain it's these two?"

Mrs. Wilson glanced at the aborigines, then bobbed her head furiously. Sebastian grinned and slowly backed into the shadows.

"It's them, all right," she answered, lifting a crooked finger as her nephew had done. "Those two. I saw them stealing my horses last night."

The painted aborigine dancers looked ready for a fight, but the silver-haired man said something and they held back. The little boy who had been with the aborigine leader disappeared.

"Now, then . . ." began the constable, and his horse began pulling around in circles. "Mitchell, help me with these two prisoners. You two men are under arrest."

The younger constable, a big-armed man, wasted no time in grabbing the two young aborigine men. A moment later he had their wrists handcuffed and was hurrying them out of the camp to the sound of howling and protests from the people. Only a stern warning from the aborigine leader kept the scary situation from getting worse.

"That's all there is to it." Constable Fitzgerald nodded at Mrs.

Wilson. "I'll accompany you home now while Mitchell attends to the prisoners." Then he turned to his deputy. "You go ahead, Mitchell. We'll be along shortly."

It had all happened so fast. Will and several of his gang remained as the fire burned down in the stunned aborigine camp. By the way the aborigines stared at them, they were obviously not welcome. Will jumped and yelled when a dirt clod sailed out of the darkness and hit him squarely on the chest.

"Who did that?" shouted Will, waving his club. He didn't wait for an answer but stepped up to a group of small boys at the edge of the camp and yanked one of them up by the arm. He looked like the same little boy who had stood next to the leader.

"You can't do that—" Patrick wanted to say from his hiding place, but all he could manage was a breathless gasp. The boy howled and kicked, and everyone started shouting. Before Patrick knew where his legs were taking him, he had turned away from the fight and sprinted back toward the river and the waiting rowboat. He plugged his ears as he ran wildly through the bushes, humming as loudly as he could manage in an attempt to block out everything except the humming sound itself. Tree branches and bushes lashed at his sides as he ran.

I don't want to hear it, he told himself, trying not to imagine what would happen in the fight. *And I definitely don't want to see it*.

But he couldn't plug his eyes at the same time, couldn't stop the sight of the boy who looked like Michael, the one with the innocent face and the big, smiling eyes.

It's not right, he thought. *Those bullies can't get away with hurting that little boy*.

When he unplugged his ears for a moment, he noticed a sound in the bush ahead of him. A horse maybe, and for a moment he thought it was the two constables returning to town with their prize. But a different voice came from the darkness.

"Good job, kid," said one of the voices, too soft to recognize. "We'll be looking for more, now that we have this settled."

And then Patrick was standing nearly face-to-face with Sebastian Weatherby.

Sebastian's eyes widened when he saw Patrick, but only for a moment. He looked quickly over his shoulder, but Patrick saw only shadows.

"Uh, sorry," mumbled Patrick, backing up slowly. "I'll just be moving on. . . ." He tripped over a root and tried to pick himself up, but Sebastian was too quick. The older boy sprang on Patrick like a cat on a mouse.

"Get off me!" protested Patrick, but Sebastian's knees dug into his ribs. The best Patrick could do was squirm on his back helplessly in the dirt.

"What are you doing out here?" growled Sebastian.

"Just walking." Patrick could hardly breathe, let alone answer.

"Walking, eh? You ought to be home in bed instead of out here spying around."

Patrick tried to get up again, but Sebastian held firm.

"Sure, and I'd be there by now," grunted Patrick, "if you weren't sitting on me."

Sebastian gave Patrick an extra shove with his knees before he got to his feet. Patrick rolled and scrambled away.

"I didn't do anything to you," Patrick managed before he started to cough.

"Never mind," hissed Sebastian. "You just stay away from these horse-thieving darkies, understand?"

Patrick put his hands on his hips. "Why do *you* care? I've a right to be here, same as anyone else."

At first Patrick didn't know what hit him. But Sebastian's lightning-fast swing caught him in a blow to the chin. With his teeth rattling, Patrick staggered a few steps backward and gripped his jaw.

"Does that help you understand?" asked Sebastian. "No one comes out here from now on. Not you. Not your sister, either."

Now I'm glad she didn't come along, thought Patrick.

"Understand?" roared Sebastian.

"I understand," Patrick finally whispered as he scrambled away.

But he didn't understand, *couldn't* understand. After what he had just seen at the aborigine camp, Patrick wasn't quite sure of anything. Horse thieves? Was it true?

Patrick didn't waste any time as he crashed through the bush. He paused for a moment to catch his breath and listened to the bullfrogs in the dark. That would lead him home.

"Don't stop now," he told himself.

He soon made it back to his waiting rowboat at the muddy bank of the Murray River. Still gasping for air, he tumbled onto the seat, pushed off, and grabbed for the oars.

"What was I doing over there?" he asked himself once more as he rowed quickly across the swollen river to his home. His jaw throbbed, and he could hear his heart thumping wildly. The weak light from a hide-and-seek moon behind the clouds seemed to break into a thousand pieces on the face of the river as Patrick pulled across.

On the opposite side Patrick could see a dim, yellow light coming from the window of the odd little cabin his grandfather let them stay in, the place his grandfather called "Erin's Landing" because of their Irish roots.

"Aaron?" the kids at school had teased him more than once. "Like Moses and Aaron in the Old Testament?"

Patrick remembered how he'd had to tell them over and over that Erin was the ancient name for Ireland. *"E-r-i-n"*, he'd repeated. "Not *A-a-r-o-n.*"

No matter what we call this place, we're still a long way from Erin, he told himself as he neared the front door and noticed the outline of his mother against the light.

"Patrick Ian McWaid," pronounced Mrs. McWaid as Patrick tried to slip in through the front door. "Have you been across the river?"

When he heard all three of his names, Patrick figured that he would not be welcomed home with open arms. Had it been an hour? Longer? He gulped.

"Did Becky tell you I was out exploring?" He tried his best to catch his breath and sound casual. "You said we weren't going to eat until later, until Pa got back from town."

"Neighbor gave me a ride home," said their father. He rose slowly from a chair in the corner of the room and ran his fingers through a well-trimmed but still curly red beard.

"But look at your pants!" His mother wiped her hands on her apron and wouldn't let Patrick pass by her. "Your knees are completely muddy and probably ripped, besides. Honestly, sometimes you're worse than Michael. I thought when you turned thirteen a few weeks ago you were finally growing out of that sort of thing!"

"I'm sorry, Ma." Patrick picked up a wash basin and headed back outside. "I'll clean up before we eat."

"It's not that." Patrick's father held the door. "We don't want you out there wandering around after dark—even if you *are* older now. You need to stay closer to the house."

His father was not extremely tall, but he was starting to get his strength back after weeks of treatment for malaria. There was no arguing with Pa when he spoke like that.

"Yes, sir," answered Patrick, stopping at the door.

"John, you should rest now," protested their mother. "You shouldn't have been out today, considering what the doctor said."

"Well, now, a man has to find a job, does he not?" Mr. McWaid smiled. "And we're speaking about the oldest son, here, not about my former illness."

"Former? Now, John, you can't be saying you're completely well already. . . ."

Patrick looked back at Becky, who frowned as she followed him outside. When his parents argued, they always seemed to sound a little more Irish, and for a moment it reminded Patrick of when they used to live in Dublin. His father would come home from working late once in a while, and his mother would fret, but only until Pa took her in his arms.

"What did you see?" Becky whispered at him. Inside, she had just set the table for a late supper of thick potato soup, fried Murray cod, and onions. Patrick figured their eight-year-old brother, Michael, must still be outside. He was probably playing with his pet koala, Christopher.

"Well?" Becky prodded.

"I'd better not tell you."

"What are you talking about?" When Becky looked more closely at him, Patrick knew he couldn't keep much of a secret from her.

"Becky, it was horrible!" In a jumbled flood of words, Patrick told his sister all that had happened—even the part about meeting Sebastian and the mysterious rider on the way home. She listened to his story with wide eyes.

"Michael!" their mother shouted out the door at the bright moon, which was hiding halfway behind a cloud. "Dinner's almost ready!"

Becky didn't move. "And you saw that Will fellow attack the aborigines?" she asked, sounding as if she didn't quite believe the story.

Patrick gritted his teeth together and looked at the ground. "Not directly. But he started to. . . ."

"But what could you have done to stop him?" asked his sister, thinking it over. "You're only thirteen, remember."

Patrick frowned. "Seems as if I should have been able to do *something*. But I just ran."

"Did the constable see you?"

Patrick shook his head. "I don't think so. He left before it all happened."

"Who left, Patrick?" asked Michael, coming around the corner of the cabin.

Patrick jumped but didn't turn around to face his brother.

"Michael, how many times have I told you not to sneak up on me like that? You'll kill me of a fright."

"No, I won't." Michael twirled on his heel but would not be put off, and he wrinkled his little button nose when they paraded back into the cabin. In his face he looked a bit like Patrick and Becky, mainly because his green eyes sparkled just like theirs. But he was darker and had his own round build, not like anyone else in the family. He put his hands on his hips and imitated their mother.

"Well?" Michael asked again. "Tell me what you saw out there. Did you see any darkies?"

"Michael!" Their mother faced her youngest directly. "Wherever did you hear that horrible word?"

For a moment Michael looked shocked, as if he hadn't understood what he had done or said to deserve that kind of reaction from his mother. He took a step backward.

"That's what the boys in town say, Ma. I was just—"

"I don't care what the boys in town say." Mrs. McWaid held up her hand. "That's a very rude name that we don't use in our family. How would you like being called such a thing? You will call them aborigines, or you will call them by their Christian names, or . . . or whatever names they now have."

Michael nodded seriously. "I heard another boy say his pa used to go out and hunt the . . . aborigines. Said they don't have souls."

Mr. McWaid shook his head sadly as he took his place at the table. "That's just not so, Michael. They're people Jesus died for, just like He died for you and me. Don't let anyone tell you different."

At the dinner table Patrick's mind wandered while his father prayed, and he imagined again the strange, almost eerie hunting dance he had watched. The odd singing. The little boys and girls. Then the arrest of the two aborigines. He sat with his hands together under the table, trying to keep them from shaking.

Why would they steal horses anyway? he wondered. *And why was Will so mean to them?*

"Eat some fish, Patrick." His mother held out a steaming plate after his father finished saying grace.

Patrick nodded and forked up a piece of the tender white fish. But he didn't join the conversation. He just chewed and stared out the dark kitchen window. His mother had framed it with a cheery blue-checkered curtain to match the rest of her tiny but clean kitchen. On the wall she had arranged a couple of blue-speckled plates on a narrow shelf—all that was left of her dishes from Ireland. Everything else had either broken or been sold to help raise money for their passage to Australia.

As Patrick stared out the window, his mind wandered back to the fine kitchen they'd had back home. Or at least it seemed fine, compared to the place they had now. But the linens, the silverware, the china—except for the two plates—were all gone. Patrick sighed. The old memories didn't seem real anymore. They had been crowded out by new sights and sounds, like the strange people dancing in the bush. The ones who were horse thieves, maybe. And bullies like Sebastian Weatherby and his friends.

"Where are ye, lad?" his father finally asked him. "You're looking a hundred miles away."

"What?" mumbled Patrick. "Oh . . ." He couldn't imagine telling the rest of his family what he had seen.

"Patrick?" His mother gave Mr. McWaid a worried glance, then set the potato soup down in front of Patrick. He started to eat but nearly burned his tongue.

Forget what you saw, he commanded himself, watching the steam rise from his bowl. *It's too late. You can't do anything about it.*

"Is anything bothering you?" His father wrinkled his brow and looked at Patrick more closely.

"I'm fine," replied Patrick, passing the onions to his brother. The words fell flat. Patrick struggled to keep his dinner down in the silence that followed.

Oh no, he thought, still keeping his shaking hand under the table. *Now my stomach isn't cooperating, either*.

Again his mind wandered, and he tried to keep from imagining what might have happened to the aborigines who had been left behind at the corroboree. *Could I really have done anything to stop the fighting?* he asked himself.

Someone pounded on the door.

"Please!" cried a boy, only it sounded more like "pliz." There was a thud against the door.

"Please help me," cried the voice.

CHAPTER 3

SAFE HAVEN

When Patrick's father pulled open the door, his mother leaped to the hunched figure of a small, dark-skinned boy.

"My dear," cried Mrs. McWaid, "are you all right?"

The young boy only moaned and looked at them with terrified eyes. His soaking-wet shirt was ripped, and his dark, curly hair lay wet and matted to his shoulders. It took just a moment for Patrick to realize it was the same boy who had been whispering to the dance leader back at the aborigine camp. The one Will had been ready to hit with his club.

"Why are you here?" asked their mother, and then it was all too clear. Patrick had to look away from the gash just above the little boy's eye.

"Quickly, get him in here," commanded their father, and suddenly their little cabin became a hospital. Patrick heated up water while Becky made a place for the patient on the bed. Michael even helped by bringing in extra firewood.

"What happened?" asked their father, dabbing at the wound with a clean shirt he had ripped into rags. The boy could only sputter a stream of words in his own language, and it was soon clear that he had used up his English words in the first moment he met them.

Mr. McWaid gently asked the boy a question, a couple of words in the aborigine language. Patrick knew it was a question, but he had never heard his father say such a thing. The aborigine's eyes grew wider, and he answered back in a tumble of strange words.

"Oh no, wait, wait." Mr. McWaid put up his hand and shook his head. "I don't understand. Too fast."

He leaned his head to the side as the boy spoke, this time more slowly.

"He says something about a white man with a club who must have hit him. Somebody else dragged off two of their young men."

"I didn't know you could understand all that," said Michael.

"Just a word here and there. You forget where I spent the last several months before you found me," their father answered. "Aborigines helped keep me alive when I was hiding out in the bush. Now it's our turn to help them."

Patrick understood what his father meant. He, too, had almost forgotten how Mr. McWaid had survived after he had escaped from prison—before they found him and he was proven innocent. But his father wasn't one to talk about himself much.

"But how can we help—" began Mrs. McWaid.

The boy continued and Mr. McWaid translated as best he could.

"Why did he come here?" asked Becky. "What's his name?"

"The little fellow says his name is Davey. Got himself in the middle of a fight and was hit on the head. The aborigines either sent him for help or he ran for his life, swam across the river, and saw our light on. But why he would trust us, I'm not sure."

Patrick gulped at his father's words but said nothing. He knew exactly what had happened to the little boy and wondered who else might have been injured. He bit his lip to keep from shaking.

"We're going to have to sew this wound up ourselves," Mr. McWaid declared. "I don't know if the doctor in town makes a practice of caring for aborigines. In the morning I'm going to see the constable about this."

Becky kneeled next to the little boy and held his hands as her father did his best to clean and stitch the wound.

"We'll help you, little fellow," she whispered, and his eyelids fluttered. Patrick stood back, afraid to come any closer.

"Shh." Becky calmed him with her voice. "No one's going to hurt you, Davey, I promise. No one's going to hurt you anymore. I won't let them. I promise."

At the sound of his name, the little boy looked up at Becky as if she were his mother. He smiled weakly and fell asleep.

Patrick was in a deep sleep the next morning when they heard another rap on the door. But this one was more impatient, and the person outside their door cleared his throat loudly before knocking again.

"McWaid, are you in there?" asked a man who started to push his way inside. From across the room Patrick saw the boy huddled on the floor. The gray early morning light caught him in the face, and Constable Alexander Fitzgerald from Echuca backed up a step.

"Oh," he sucked in his breath. "I didn't know you had a visitor."

Patrick stood behind his parents as they met the lawman. Davey sat up on his blanket on the floor, shielding his eyes from the sun. When he saw the constable, he backed away on his knees in fear.

"Constable Fitzgerald," began their father, not noticing the boy's reaction, "I was going to come see you this morning. But what brings you out here?"

Constable Fitzgerald's eyebrows arched curiously, and he leaned his wide shoulders around the human shield Patrick's parents had put between the aborigine boy and the outside world.

"I've got two unhappy gully-rakers in my jail this morning," replied the constable. Patrick could tell that he spent plenty of time polishing the silver buttons on his dark blue uniform. "Couple of aborigines. They were with that bunch camped over there on the other side of the river."

"What's a gully-raker?" Michael poked his head around his mother's skirt to stare up at the constable.

The constable chuckled for a moment, then caught himself and settled back into his serious glare. "Gully-raker's a cattle thief, or in this case, a horse thief. These two were positively identified by a concerned citizen just last night."

Concerned citizen, thought Patrick, and the picture of Sebastian Weatherby and his friends came to mind.

"So who's this?" asked the constable, looking around Mrs. McWaid at their aborigine guest. Mr. McWaid crossed his arms.

"He came to us for help last night. A mob of young toughs from town came and attacked him and his people, from what I understand. Some kind of vigilante mob, taking the law into their own hands. I thought we didn't do things like that around here."

The constable took a deep breath and puffed up his chest.

"Now, you know I only want to do what's proper and lawful. 'Twas no vigilantism going on, I'll assure you."

Mr. McWaid raised his eyebrows. "No? What about this boy, then? That's what I was going to come see you about."

"I was there myself, McWaid," insisted the constable. "And there was no violence, not while I was there. There's no telling how this youngster actually injured himself."

Patrick started to speak, but he held his tongue while the constable went on.

"Now, the reason I came calling this morning is to see if you or your neighbors might be able to tell me anything else about the aborigines over there. Do you, perchance, know anything about the corroboree held out there last night?"

Their father crossed his arms and looked around the room. Patrick swallowed hard and backed up against the side wall.

"You being ill, sir," continued the constable, "I'd not expect you to be out and about. But the boy?"

Mr. McWaid looked curiously at Patrick. "You didn't go far last evening before dinner, did you, son?"

Patrick wondered for a moment what would happen if he said no. Only Becky would know better, and she wouldn't tell, would she?

"Uh, just for a while," answered Patrick.

His father studied his face. "Hear anything about one of those aborigine corroborees?"

"Does he know what a corroboree is?" asked the constable.

Patrick finally nodded. "I know. I was there."

"You were *what*?" Patrick's father turned to face his son, his mouth open in amazement.

"I went out walking." Patrick knew it was too late to hide anything. "I wanted to know what the funny sounds were."

"And?" Constable Fitzgerald leaned forward.

The aborigine boy had collected himself and looked from person to person with big eyes. When he looked at the constable, though, he dared only to stare at his shiny silver badge.

"I found them not far from the river," Patrick reported. "They were singing and playing their instruments. It was really interesting."

"And a dance?" The constable sounded as if he was looking for a particular clue. "What kind of dance?"

"Uh . . ." When Patrick closed his eyes, he could still see dancers, the ones with their spears. "Some kind of hunting dance."

"Come now, Constable," protested Mrs. McWaid. "Surely this has nothing to do with—"

"Citizens I've spoken with were extremely disturbed by the dance," interrupted the constable. "It's very important, boy. Tell me about the dance."

"It was a hunting dance," Patrick finally blurted out. "They were just acting out some kind of hunt."

"A hunt for settlers' animals?" The constable leaned forward like a judge, his eyes intense and drilling.

Patrick had to look away. He shrugged. "I don't know. Could have been, but later—"

"That's exactly what Will and his friends told me," interrupted Constable Fitzgerald. He rocked back on his heels with a smile. "But I wanted to hear it from another witness. You've been very helpful."

"But, sir," Patrick tried once more. "What about the little boy? Someone hit him on the head."

The constable shook his head. "I told you already there's nothing to concern you. That will be the end of it."

Mrs. McWaid wasn't smiling. "Patrick, why didn't you tell us any of this last night?" she asked.

Patrick studied a crack in the wood floor and could think of no answer.

"Sounds to me as if he's been very helpful, if I may say so, Mrs. McWaid." The constable bowed slightly as he backed away from the front door. "His testimony about the aborigines will certainly help keep those two gully-rakers in jail, where they belong. G'day to you."

Patrick glanced again at Davey, and he was sure the boy hadn't understood a word they had said. Still, Davey looked nervously back up at them.

If he only knew, thought Patrick. Everyone except Davey followed the constable outside; he stopped and turned before climbing back on his waiting horse.

"Oh, one other thing, McWaid. You know a little of the aborigine babble, don't you?" He didn't wait for Mr. McWaid to answer. "I was wondering if you could come down to the jail and translate a few things for us from those two darkies."

Patrick saw his father wince at the constable's choice of words. The lawman continued. "Perhaps take a statement or two from them before they're tried. Just a formality."

Mr. McWaid nodded, and the constable disappeared down the lane.

"You should have told us, son," said Patrick's father as he sighed and leaned back against the cabin's outside wall for support. His mother held his arm.

"John," she told him gently, "you're not as well as you think you are. Come back inside and sit down. I'll fix you a bite to eat."

Mr. McWaid didn't move, only stared off in the distance. From back inside the cabin, they heard a rustling and a window opening.

"Davey!" cried Becky, turning around. "Don't go!"

CHAPTER 4

HARD LESSON

The bedroll on the floor where the aborigine boy had slept was empty.

"Do you think he understood some of what we were saying after all?" Patrick asked his sister as they ran around to the back of the cabin, the side facing the river.

Becky shook her head as they hurried down to the water. "Must have been the sight of the constable that scared him off," she replied.

"Well, whatever spooked him, he climbed out that window pretty quickly."

They stood for a moment on the riverbank, watching the cold brown water flow by. Here and there a whirlpool broke the surface, showing off its power as if it were flexing a muscle. This time of year, the rainy season, even Patrick would think twice before swimming across. But it looked as if that was the only direction their little aborigine friend could have gone, and they stood watching for a moment.

"There he is, see?" Michael pointed to a log about halfway across the river. "He's pushing that log across, using it for a float."

Patrick finally caught sight of the boy, and they watched quietly for a few minutes before he finally made it to the other side. Patrick put his hands to his mouth to yell, but his sister caught his arm.

"Don't," she told him, and Davey looked their way for a minute. They could only stare at him as he crawled out of the water and disappeared into the bush.

"I hope he's all right," worried Becky.

"He'll be fine," replied their father. "I'm just worried there will be more fighting."

I should have done something to stop it, Patrick told himself. *And I should have convinced the constable. If only I hadn't run away last night* . . .

He knew he wasn't being realistic to think he could have done anything. But he couldn't shake the nagging feeling—even while he kept busy washing clothes and chopping wood that Saturday afternoon. Mr. McWaid wrote a letter to give to the owner of the newspaper in town—in hopes of getting a job there. And after dinner Pa pulled out the family Bible to read to them, the same way he had done back in Dublin.

"You read it this time, Patrick," his father asked him, relaxing in a wooden chair by the stone fireplace. "My eyes are starting to give out." Their fire crackled warmly and Patrick's eyes were used to the flickering light, but he didn't take the book from his father right away.

"What's the matter, Patrick?" His mother put down a dish she was polishing and felt his forehead. "You're not sick, are you, now? You always want to be the first to read."

"I'm not sick." Patrick took the worn, black leather book and noted where his father had pointed out for him to read. He cleared his throat and looked at the top of the page.

"James chapter four, verse thirteen," he read. " 'Go to now, ye that say, To day or to morrow we will go into such a city, and continue there a year, and buy and sell, and get gain. . . .' "

The fire popped cheerily as the occasional stray raindrop splashed against the tiny front window. To Patrick the room felt too quiet.

"Go on," his father urged him.

" 'Whereas ye know not what shall be on the morrow. For what is your life? It is even a vapor, that appeareth for a little time, and then vanisheth away.' "

"Are we really a vapor?" asked Michael, looking up from the wooden top he was spinning on the floor.

Their father chuckled. He looked at Patrick in the dimness of the cabin, and his warm eyes told Patrick to keep reading.

" '. . . Ye ought to say, If the Lord will, we shall live, and do this, or that.' "

Michael giggled. Becky frowned at their little brother, and Patrick pulled the big book closer as it grew even darker inside the cabin.

"Let him read, Michael," said Becky. Patrick took another breath.

" 'Therefore to him that knoweth to do good, and doeth it not, to him it is sin.' "

Again Patrick paused and looked around the room, the final words of the Scripture echoing in his head. *To him that knoweth to do good, and doeth it not . . .*

"Is that enough?" he asked.

His father didn't open his eyes. "For now."

"One good thing about school, lately," Becky began as they stepped out of the little wooden school building Monday afternoon.

"What's that?" asked Patrick, checking to make sure he had his books with him.

"Well, Sebastian Weatherby isn't there to bother you anymore. Not since he quit coming to class."

Patrick nodded. He knew all too well that Echuca's number one bully was still in town, which was bad enough in itself. But at least they didn't have to face Sebastian every day, the way they had for the first few weeks they attended classes in Echuca.

"It just annoys me that all the adults in town think he and Will are such gentlemen," said Becky, adjusting her load of books.

"I guess adults don't see what he's really like," agreed Patrick. "He even had Miss Tyler fooled."

By now they were pretty much used to Miss Tyler and what took place in her one-room school. And if it didn't include Sebastian, well, that was fine with Patrick.

His sister didn't seem to mind, either. But she stopped for a moment, her hands on her hips. "What happened to Michael?" she wondered. "I thought he was going to wait for us."

Patrick shrugged, remembering that some of the younger kids had been dismissed a half hour earlier. "He probably got impatient and is home by now."

As they continued on, Patrick glanced over at a group of boys in a vacant lot between two buildings. One was standing with his back to them with a kind of flat bat on his shoulder, waiting for another player to throw a ball at him.

"I didn't know they played cricket around here," said Patrick, pausing to watch the wide-shouldered boy slap the ball far over everyone's head. "I thought it was an English gentleman's game."

"I didn't think so, either," replied Becky. "But obviously they've changed the rules to suit them." Like Patrick, she had only seen the game played once or twice. It wasn't an Irish sport.

They heard a crack of a bat, then the ball bounced hard off the side of a building. A moment later a man with a smudged white apron came running out the front door of the shop, waving his hands.

"Hey!" yelled the shopkeeper. "How many times . . ." His voice trailed off when he saw who was standing in the field next to the shop. "Oh, Sebastian, it's you."

"Terribly sorry, Mr. Worthington, sir." Sebastian Weatherby grinned and made a show of bowing to the shopkeeper, who smiled back and shook his head patiently. "We'll be more careful next time."

But when Mr. Worthington turned to go back inside, Sebastian made his friends laugh by sticking his tongue out at the shopkeeper.

They all think he's so wonderful, fumed Patrick. He and Becky stood back against the side of the newspaper office and tried to stay out of sight when Sebastian trotted toward them.

Sebastian saw Becky and lifted his black cap in greeting. "G'day, Miss Becky," he said with a smile, but it turned into a cold glare when he spotted Patrick.

Patrick stood rooted to his spot after Sebastian and the cricket players left. Becky tugged on his arm. "Come on," she told him. "Pa said he would meet us at the newspaper office. Think he'll get that part-time job?"

"Probably." Patrick closed his eyes and imagined for a moment what it would be like if they could all just go back home to Dublin. No more muddy streets. No more trouble with the aborigines. No more Sebastian and Will. . . .

But it would cost a fearsome amount of money to return, their father had told them, and besides, wouldn't they want to be part of an exciting, growing young country like Australia? Their father had hinted more than once that they might be staying. But Patrick couldn't figure out why his father didn't seem to miss Dublin the way he did.

Patrick was still walking and daydreaming when he heard Becky gasp. He looked up to see her reading a copy of the latest *Riverine Herald*, which was posted in the office window for passers-by to read.

"Patrick . . . look here. Quickly." Patrick joined her to see what had caught her attention.

"What's this?" he asked, and he couldn't help groaning when he saw the story with a large headline on the front page.

" 'More Horse Thefts,' " he read quietly. " 'A local youth's testimony has confirmed the shocking possibility that a recent gathering of aborigines may have been planning yet another raid on area livestock. Two suspected thieves were taken into custody with the help of vigilant Echuca citizens.' "

"You were there, Patrick," said Becky quietly. "Do you really think those two aborigines stole that woman's horses?"

Patrick thought for a moment. "I don't know. It looks like it, but . . . oh, Becky, I just don't know what to say either way."

He sighed, and they heard voices even before they pushed open the door next to the window with the carefully painted gold letters: *The Riverine Herald, est. 1863.*

"There he is." Patrick's father pointed at him, and Patrick almost turned right around and headed back out the door. Becky stopped short, as well.

Their father must have seen the expression on their faces, because he stood right up and waved them over to where a man in an ink-stained shirt and black trousers sat behind a desk.

"Certainly, Mr. Field. My point is that if you had a trained reporter on your staff, you might have been able to speak directly to the people involved. My son, here, for example, was the one who saw the aborigine dance. The one you mentioned in the front-page story."

Mr. W. Sterling Field, the man with the engraved brass nameplate on his desk, nodded at their father through a thick cloud of horrible blue pipe smoke. Patrick hung back, wondering how he was going to breathe.

"And surely you agree, sir," continued their father, patting Patrick on the back, "that it's better to report direct quotes, that is, speak directly to the people involved? It's simply a matter of journalistic integrity—"

"Yes, of course, of course." Mr. Field sat up straight in his leather chair. "Believe me, I appreciate your perspective. But perhaps you don't know how absolutely terrified the townspeople are of these dark—" Mr. Field nodded at Becky and Patrick from behind a mountain of paper that covered his desk. "I should say, aborigines. Do you realize the fear connected to the image of dark savages with spears? It's not right, I grant you. But people just don't know what they'll do next. . . ."

While the two men continued, Patrick and Becky looked around. The *Riverine Herald* was like the office where their father had once worked in Dublin. Except here paper covered the floor almost as thickly as the smoke around Mr. Field's desk, and the sharp aroma of ink mixed with the pipe smoke. In the corner a stooped older man sat in front of a table full of trays, each filled with metal letter stamps of different sizes. He looked like he was putting together a puzzle.

"Have you ever seen a typesetter before?" A pleasant-looking older woman looked up at them from another desk.

Patrick and Becky both nodded as the man jockeyed trays of letters together into place. Later the trays of metal letters, called galleys, would be clamped together to form entire pages of type for the printing press.

"This is just like the office back home where father worked," Patrick replied. "Only smaller."

"Oh, I should have known. You're the children of that Irish gentleman who's here for a reporter's job." She gave them a wink. "Goodness knows Mr. Field needs the help. With his regular reporter gone for a while, he's practically been doing it all himself."

Patrick smiled at the woman and noticed the latest issue of the *Herald* on the table next to her desk. He was almost afraid to look at the article on the aborigines, the one where the constable had told everyone about Patrick seeing the hunting dance. Becky picked it up.

"What's the name of the woman whose horses were stolen?" Becky asked as she fingered the paper.

The woman looked up from her ledger book, putting the tip of her pencil down in the middle of a column of numbers she was adding.

"Ruth Wilson." She pointed at the article. "Poor Ruth, she lost her husband last year, and now all this. It's a downright shame, it is. She's all alone, lives on a little farm just south of town, near the river."

As the woman went on about how terrible Ruth Wilson's life was, Patrick noticed a giant book of old newspapers bound together in a single volume as a kind of reference book. He opened it and scanned the headlines from two, three, and four years ago: floods, stagecoach holdups, new paddle steamers launched on the river . . . His eye jumped to a name in the middle of one of the articles.

"Randolph Wilson," he said, pointing to an article from two

years ago about a boy who had won a local spelling bee. "Is this person from the same family?"

The woman pushed her chair back, then stepped over to where Patrick was standing. She leaned over and fixed her half glasses to her nose, then squinted at the report.

"That would be Ruth's nephew, her half-sister's son." She adjusted the glasses on her nose before continuing. "Little Will, everyone used to call him. Now it's just plain Will. Sharp fellow, this Will. I expect he'll find himself mayor of the city someday."

Little Will, thought Patrick, and he remembered the name from the aborigine camp. Will, the big, blond-haired leader of the toughs who had raided the corroboree. Patrick finished the article, closed the big book of newspapers, and stood back when a man burst into the office and brushed right by them. He left the door hanging wide open.

"He's at it again!" bellowed the man. "Constable's already down there, if you want to cover the story."

"Who's at it again?" asked Mr. Field, putting down his pipe.

"George the fisherman," answered the man. "He's crazy, he is, starting fights at the bank now."

Mr. Field groaned, then brightened as he looked at Mr. McWaid. "There's your first story, McWaid, if you're feeling up to it. Go see what old George is upset about this time. Just remember, the job's yours only until my regular man returns."

Patrick's father took a notebook from an empty desk and smiled as he looked at Patrick and Becky.

"Well, kids, looks as if I'll be getting to work a little sooner than anyone thought." He paused for a moment to hold on to the corner of the desk.

"Pa?" asked Becky, stepping to her father's side. He held out his hand, signaling he was all right.

"I'm fine." He stood up straight. "Now, I'll tell you what. Go on home without me, and you tell your mother I'll be home a bit later tonight. Seven o'clock, at the latest. Can you do that?"

"Pa, we're not little anymore." Patrick crossed his arms. "Can't we go see what's happening?"

"Absolutely not." Their father smiled and messed up Patrick's hair. "This doesn't concern you children. Now, don't forget to tell your mother."

He gently pushed them out the front door, then turned left and hurried down the street toward the center of town. Becky looked the other way.

"Well, are you coming?" she asked Patrick.

"Coming where?"

"We're going to talk to Ruth Wilson."

"Ruth Wilson?" Patrick dug in his heels. "Why would we want to do that?"

"She's the only one who can tell us more about what happened the night her horses were taken."

"Wait a minute, Becky. Let's just leave it alone. I don't think we had better . . ."

Becky didn't turn around; she was already hurrying down the street, away from town. Patrick sighed.

"Becky! Wait!"

It certainly wasn't a "farm," the way Patrick remembered farms back home in Ireland, where farms had ancient, whitewashed cottages with thatched straw roofs, and neat, orderly green fields on rolling hillsides, separated by fences that had been standing since the time of the Romans. Patrick stared at the place in front of him.

More like a shack in the middle of an overgrown field.

Patrick paused with his sister at Ruth Wilson's gate, which barely clung to the sorry-looking rail fence that circled the property. A goat with its ribs showing grazed in the middle of the weed-choked meadow, tied carelessly by a thin rope to the only small tree on the property. Patrick took one look at the oversized black-and-brown dog on the narrow front porch of the cottage and stood his ground.

"I'm not going in there with that monster," he declared. The hair on the back of the monster's neck raised in response. And even from across the yard Patrick noticed its fine collection of pearly white teeth.

"Good protection for a widow." Becky touched the gate—which fell off at the hinges—and the dog sprang into action.

"Becky!" warned Patrick, grabbing his sister's arm.

"Oh dear." Becky held out her hand as the dog charged.

CHAPTER 5

SHADOW WOMAN'S STORY

Patrick knew it was no good to run, but it was no good for both of them to be eaten, either, so he tried to step out in front of his sister and find a stick. Just before the dog was upon them, Patrick noticed that one of its eyes was sky-blue and the other dark brown, which gave the mongrel an off-balance, crazy sort of look. Patrick yelled, "Get away!" but the dog didn't seem to hear.

Then, as if yanked backward by an invisible leash, the dog suddenly stopped a few steps from Patrick and Becky and growled.

"Nice dog." Patrick took a deep breath and quickly let go of his sister's arm. He heard a whistle from the shadows of the shack, and the dog obediently turned around and trotted back to his master.

"Get back here, Hannibal." The voice sounded old and tired. The dog turned his head as if listening to every word, though no one stepped out into the afternoon light.

"Excuse me," Becky called out to the shadow. The dog finally curled up outside the door, its blue eye fixed on their every move. "We're looking for Ruth Wilson. Do you—"

"You found her," interrupted the shadow. "What do you want?"

"We just wanted to talk for a minute." Becky sounded very adult. "Actually, I wanted to ask you a question. It's about the other night. Thursday night, when your horses were stolen."

42

The person in the shadows said nothing for a long moment, as if she was thinking it over.

"Would that be all right?" Becky tried once more.

The shadow moved away from the door.

"He won't bite, if that's what you're worried about."

Patrick took that as an invitation to come in, so they stepped over the gate and tiptoed up the overgrown gravel path between two red oleander bushes, tired and flowerless in the topsy-turvy Australian winter month of August. Out in the yard to his right, he could barely make out a little stone angel statue that was covered in vines and meadow grass the goat couldn't reach. The cabin itself looked like a forgotten cave, overgrown like the statue with meadow grass all the way up to its windowsills. Each window was covered by a dirty, dark shade, drawn all the way down. Patrick held his breath as they stepped inside and their eyes adjusted to the darkness.

"*Sit!*" barked the shadow woman.

Patrick couldn't tell if the command was meant for them or for the dog, but they obeyed. So did the animal. Patrick hurriedly felt his way to a single upright wooden chair and perched on the nearest corner. Becky balanced on the other corner.

Finally his eyes opened wide enough to make out the outline of their hostess rocking steadily in a rocking chair that squealed with each move. The dog's claws clicked across the bare wood floor, until next to the rocker Patrick could see the single blue eye of the guard dog and a long pink tongue bobbing in the dimness.

Becky cleared her throat and slowly stood again. "I'm Becky McWaid, and this is my brother Patrick."

The rocking chair squeaked, and the room smelled like dog breath.

"We haven't lived here long." Becky tried another way to warm up the conversation. "We were curious about a story we read in today's paper."

Still the rocking chair squeaked.

If she lets that dog go, Patrick worried, keeping one foot pointed toward the door, *I'm running*.

"It was about you," Becky finished hopefully. "Or actually, about the horses stolen from you."

The chair stopped. A chicken strutted into the room from a back door, and the woman made no move to stop it.

"What do you know about it?" The woman's voice was softer this time, and she leaned forward far enough for them to see her face. It was the same woman Patrick had seen that night at Dingo Creek, all right, only she looked much older up close. By the filtered light that made it through her shredded curtains and dirty windows, Patrick could see her face was wrinkled with worry lines, and her hair was pulled back into a neat gray bun. She may have once been very pretty, but Patrick was sure that had been long ago.

"Nothing," put in Patrick. "But we were just wondering—"

"We were wondering," interrupted Becky, "if you actually saw the aborigines you say stole your horses."

The woman in the rocking chair stared at them cautiously. "Did anyone say I didn't see them?"

"It's not that," answered Becky. "We just thought—"

"Well, I saw them with my own two eyes, just the way I told that young constable—what's his name?"

"Fitzgerald," answered Becky.

"Yes, Fitzgerald. Do you know him?"

Becky nodded once.

"Well, just like I was telling the constable when he first came to ask questions, I told him I saw those two young black fellows at the edge of my field the other night." She pointed out the door. "They were dragging the animals away, just as bold as you please, and those being the only horses I have. Richard left them to me. . . ."

Patrick guessed that Richard had been the woman's husband.

"So you're sure you recognized them?" wondered Patrick.

"Why, of course I did. Raised them both since they were colts, I did. Champion stock, and you can't confuse my horses with any others. One's black as night, with a spot of day on his shoulder. And his sister's the same way, only she has white hooves."

"No, no," interrupted Patrick. "I meant, you're positive about recognizing the aborigine fellows? The two they just brought to jail?"

The woman nodded.

"But it was dark?" asked Becky, sounding like a lawyer in a courtroom.

"As I told the young constable, the moon was on their faces. I saw them."

"Even though they were all the way on the other side of your field?"

"I still recognized them," the woman insisted. The rocking stopped and the dog tried to pull away from her grip on its neck. "It's those same two fellows they just put in the jail."

"And what about the dog?" Becky wanted to know. "Did he bark?"

Ruth Wilson stopped to think, then slowly shook her head. "I don't recall that part."

"You really don't remember?" Patrick tried once again.

"Don't be impertinent," the woman snapped back. "You don't know what it's like to lose your husband and live all alone, then to have two valuable horses stolen out from under your nose, just like that."

"I'm sorry," whispered Becky.

For a moment they just sat there, until they heard a horse approach the house. The dog's ears perked up, and he shot away from Ruth's grip, almost sending her sprawling. He was across the floor with a yelp and out the door before anyone could stand up. A moment later he was back, wagging his tail.

"Hey, Aunt Ruth!" called a voice from just outside. "Anything to eat here?"

Patrick looked over at his sister and stood up. "Let's go, Becky."

"Hello?" bellowed the voice again, and by the time Patrick made it to the door, he was face-to-face with an older boy in his teens wearing a familiar ragged hunting jacket and cap.

Will stopped in the doorway, staring at Patrick, then at Becky. "What are you doing here?" he demanded of Patrick.

"Just leaving," said Patrick, slipping under the boy's arm and tripping over the chicken. "Come on, Becky."

By the time he finds out why we were here, thought Patrick as he ran through the field to the gate, *we'll be gone*.

The dog followed him, nipping at his heels before Patrick vaulted over the broken gate. Will must have leaned it back in place.

"Becky?" Patrick turned to see his sister still standing by the front door of Ruth Wilson's cottage, squinting across the meadow at him. He waved at her to follow, and she ran toward him—around the wildly barking dog.

"What were you waiting for?" he asked his sister when she had caught up.

"Just checking what I could see from the front veranda, that's all. Think she could have recognized two fellows from that distance?"

"I don't know. Maybe." Patrick looked back nervously to make sure Will wasn't following them on his horse. "But visiting her was a waste of time, don't you think?"

"Maybe not."

Patrick let it go at that, and they didn't stop until they were standing in front of the newspaper office. Outside the office, Patrick caught a faint whiff of pipe smoke, but he couldn't see his father anywhere. Becky hurried inside.

"Come on, Becky," he whispered as he drummed his fingers against a hitching rack. "He's not in there."

Inside, Becky was talking again with the woman at the front desk. A horse stopped in the street right behind Patrick, and its rider jumped to the muddy street.

"There you are. McWaid, is it?"

Patrick turned to run when he saw Will, but the only way clear was the dark, narrow space between two buildings. It was barely wide enough to fit his shoulders through, but he squeezed sideways and scrambled as quickly as he could.

"Wait!" shouted Will. "I just want to tell you . . ."

But Patrick didn't want to hear. He crashed through the narrow junkyard of broken furniture, glass, and bottles. An alley cat screamed a protest and latched on to Patrick's leg.

"Ow!" Patrick skipped along on one leg, then fell face first into a broken wooden crate full of old newspapers and bird's nests. He stumbled out the far end of the alley in a cloud of feathers, rolling to a stop in front of a pair of boots planted squarely in his path.

"Uh, excuse me." Patrick didn't want to look up, and the boots didn't move.

"Where are you going, Irish boy?" asked the person belonging to the boots. "Pretending you're a chicken?"

Patrick groaned when he heard Sebastian Weatherby's voice. Sebastian hoisted Patrick up by his shoulders and stood him against the wall of a building just as Will came charging around on his old horse.

He must have followed us after all, Patrick told himself, looking over at the the newspaper building. It wouldn't do any good for Becky to come to the rescue.

"Here he is, Will," chuckled Sebastian, still holding Patrick up by his shirt with one hand. In his other he held a cricket bat. "This the fellow you wanted to see?"

"What do you want with me?" Patrick stiffened when Will slipped down to the ground and strutted over.

"Don't worry yourself," said Sebastian, pressing Patrick into the wall even harder. "Will just wants to talk. I told him about our little chat the other night."

"I don't have anything to say to you." Patrick squirmed but couldn't get away.

Sebastian arched his eyebrows in surprise. "Well, what do you think of this, Will? Here we are, just paying him a friendly visit, and he's being rude to you, don't you think?"

Will laughed just as the back door to the *Riverine Herald* building creaked open. Sebastian backed away.

"Patrick!" cried Becky, rushing out the door. "What's going on?"

"He fell down, sister," said Sebastian, stepping forward. "We only came along to give him a hand."

Becky hesitated for a moment, but Patrick could tell she wasn't fooled for a second.

"Come on, Patrick," she told him, pulling him toward the door.

But the locked back door had slammed shut. Becky knocked, but no one came, and Sebastian stood his ground.

"We just wanted to let you know how proud we are of you," continued Sebastian. He crossed his arms contentedly while Will climbed back onto his horse.

"You know what I mean. It was in the paper, remember? Something about a local boy telling the police about the attacking aborigines? That was very good."

Patrick closed his eyes and tried to wipe away the feathers in his hair.

"And the next time you get a chance, you're going to say the same thing, right?"

Patrick had been hoping there wouldn't be a next time.

"My brother doesn't—" Becky broke in, but Sebastian stopped her with a dark stare.

"I was talking to your brother this time, pretty miss," he snapped at her. "Not you."

Patrick pounded on the door again, but still no one heard.

"Now, Irish boy, did I hear you promise you would say the right thing next time it comes up?"

The "right" thing to you, Sebastian Weatherby, isn't . . . thought Patrick, but he said nothing. *Why doesn't someone come to the door?*

"What's that?" asked Sebastian, still holding his cricket bat as he stepped forward. "I can't hear you."

"Sure," Patrick finally managed to whisper.

"Sure what?"

"I promise."

"And what do you promise?" Sebastian smacked the bat in his hand. "Let me hear you."

"I promise to say the right thing next time," Patrick said through his teeth.

"There now," Sebastian smiled and took a step back. "I just

wanted to make sure we understood each other. Wouldn't want you to be, ah, hurt by saying the wrong thing."

"Is that some kind of threat, Sebastian Weatherby?" Becky wasn't backing down from the bully, not this time.

He laughed at them and strutted toward a couple of other boys his age who had appeared at the end of the alley.

"I'd like to stay," he replied over his shoulder, "but my team needs me. Cricket, you know." Of course Becky and Patrick didn't answer.

"Complicated game, cricket. Far too complicated for you and your darkie friends, I'll wager."

He looked straight at Patrick as Will spun his horse around and galloped off. "Now, don't forget what I told you, kid. Don't want you two to get yourselves injured."

Patrick glared back at him. *Sure you don't*.

"Hey, Sebastian!" yelled one of the others from the end of the alley. "Coming?"

"Just a minute!" he hollered back. "My turn to bat!"

Patrick and Becky turned down the alley in the opposite direction.

"How *could* you, Patrick?" His sister glared at him as soon as Sebastian was out of sight. "You just told that bully what he wanted to hear!"

"He was going to break my neck with that cricket bat, Becky. You saw him."

"Did you hear what he said about aborigines? He talked about them as if they weren't even people! I thought you always stood up to those types."

"And I thought you didn't approve of fighting."

"I wasn't talking about fighting. Just saying the right thing."

"That's exactly what I promised him I would say. The right thing."

"Does that mean right for Sebastian Weatherby?" she asked. "Or just right in general?"

"I'm thinking."

"Patrick!"

"I know what you mean, Becky. I just wasn't very eager for that bully to swat me down the alley like a cricket ball. Do you know what that feels like?"

"Of course not. I just thought you weren't going to run away again, like—" She stopped herself midsentence.

"Go ahead and say it, Becky." Patrick kicked a rusty tin can down the alley as hard as he could. "You thought I wasn't going to run from Sebastian Weatherby, the way I did the other night. Well, it's just not that simple."

"I know it's not." Becky's voice softened as they walked down the street, then along the rutted wagon trail that led out of Echuca. They followed the river for a while, then cut through patches of fragrant eucalyptus, the beautiful, streaked river red gums. Patrick washed the mud off his face and shirt when they came to a low bank in the river. And they said little the rest of the two miles home.

"Do you hear something?" Becky asked a short time later when they turned down the narrow lane leading to their grandfather's cabin. Patrick was afraid they were going to be late for dinner.

"Probably just a bird." Patrick didn't stop, didn't think.

"No." Becky shook her head and hurried her step. "I know what a bird sounds like."

"What's your hurry?" asked Patrick, feeling the miles in his feet.

"I heard rustling," replied Becky, almost running now, "like someone is following us."

What now? Patrick followed his sister, but by that time she was far ahead, almost to the cabin. "Beck—" Her name was torn from his mouth as he was suddenly tackled from behind.

CHAPTER 6

UNEXPECTED GUESTS

"Oh!" Patrick hit the ground with a grunt, the wind nearly knocked out of him. He struggled to get free, kicking and squirming.

But his attacker let him go and kneeled on the ground, laughing.

"Caught you," said the attacker. He jumped up and smiled.

"Jeff!" Patrick took a deep breath as he was hauled to his feet. "I knew you'd come back. I just didn't think you'd come back to attack me."

"Thought I'd surprise you." The American boy smiled from ear to ear as he pounded Patrick on the back. He was only a couple of years older than Patrick, but bigger and broader. "Where's your sister?"

"Up ahead," explained Patrick as they hurried to the cabin. He couldn't help but smile. *Jeff is back!*

Jefferson Pitney hadn't changed any in the months since the McWaids had seen him last, when he had to return to his ship, the *Star of Africa*. He had the same square, powerful face with the boxer's nose, and the same infectious smile that made everyone around him grin. The same gentle southern drawl that made listening to his stories so much fun.

"You'll have to tell us everything," said Patrick as the front door flew open.

Becky stood frozen there for a moment, wide-eyed. "Oh!" she gasped, looking as shocked as Patrick had been. "It's you."

"Sure, it's me." Jefferson grinned for a moment before stepping up to shake hands all around.

Michael bounced up and down with excitement. "He's back, he's back, he's back!" he sang. His dark, wavy hair flopped as he jumped, and it served as the perfect handhold for Christopher. As usual, the little koala perched on Michael's shoulder.

Jefferson held up his hands. "You didn't think I'd come back?"

"I thought you had to stay on the ship," began Becky.

"Well, sure I did." Jefferson nodded. "But when I got back to the *Star of Africa*, the way I promised I would, wouldn't you know that the ship had been sold out from under us, and—"

"Sold?" interrupted Michael.

"Let him tell the story, Michael," warned their mother with a smile.

Jefferson took a deep breath and continued. "Right. It sold to an Englishman, and turns out he had his own ideas about what kind of crew he wanted. First he takes us right back to Kangaroo Island to pick up a cargo of seal skins. I figured here was my chance, so I collected my pay and left that ship for good."

"Kangaroo Island . . ." Patrick tried to put the pieces together, and his mind went back to the island just off Australia's coast where he and the American cabin boy had first washed up. It was a welcome relief after Jefferson fell overboard during a horrible storm and Patrick went in after him, diving into the shark infested ocean water. Patrick's mother and the others back on the *Star of Africa* thought he and Jefferson had surely died. Obviously they hadn't. An aborigine boy named Luke made sure of that.

"You didn't see Luke, did you?" asked Patrick.

This time it was his mother's turn to laugh as she stood watching the reunion. She glanced at the pilothouse room of their odd cabin, where their grandfather had attached the old wheelhouse of a riverboat. "Should we tell them?"

Michael's button nose turned up with the excited question, and a dark figure stepped out from around the corner of the wheelhouse room.

"Luke!" Patrick whispered as the other boy stepped into the main room of the cabin. It was really Luke, the aborigine who had fed them and who brought them to safety on Kangaroo Island.

"Surprise!" cried Michael as Patrick struggled to figure out why the two boys were both there. "They've been here an hour!" Michael skipped over and grabbed Luke's hand.

"Luke," repeated Patrick, his mouth hanging open.

Jefferson laughed and pointed at Patrick. "You look just the way Luke did when I showed up on his island."

"I just wasn't expecting—" Patrick sputtered.

"Tell them what you told us," Michael urged their aborigine friend. Luke still hung back shyly, but he certainly didn't look as he had the first time they had met, in a cave on Kangaroo Island. That time Luke had been wearing only a pair of ripped black trousers. Now he wore almost the same clothes as Jefferson: sturdy denim sailor's pants and a pullover blue jersey. And while his hair had been cut so that it didn't look as wild as before, the fourteen-year-old boy's ebony skin was as dark as Patrick remembered.

This is going to be interesting, thought Patrick.

"My aunt Bet died suddenly. Fever. Just after you left the island." Luke spoke with the sturdy English accent he had learned from the lighthouse keeper, Henry Gates, who had cared for him since he was very young.

"Oh." Patrick caught his breath and bowed his head slightly. "I'm sorry."

Luke nodded, but the awkward silence didn't last long. Outside, the sun had set and the bullfrogs down by the river were beginning their nightly concert.

"So what happened to Gates?" Patrick finally asked.

"He's still watching the light. Jefferson came and stayed for a couple of days, and Gates told me I should go with him to find you again, if I wanted. Thought the change of scenery would do me good."

The aborigine boy flashed a brilliant white smile that seemed to shut out the bad news about his aunt Bet. "And I've never been all the way up the Murray River before."

"Only thing is," put in Jefferson, "looks like we're too late. You and Becky found your pa without us. After I promised you I'd help you find him and all. You could have at least waited until I got back! Where is he, anyway?"

"Oh!" Patrick turned to his mother. "I forgot to tell you. Pa got a temporary job with the paper. He'll be home by seven."

He turned back to his friends and put his hand on Luke's shoulder. "I am very sorry about your aunt."

Luke nodded and looked around. "Me too. It was very sudden. Doctor didn't even have time to come from Kingscoate."

Tears brimmed over in Luke's dark eyes, and he wiped them away with the sleeve of his loose-fitting sailor's shirt. Again, no one spoke for a moment.

"Then Jefferson came. I didn't think I would ever see him again. *You*, maybe, but not the boy from Arkansas."

Jefferson shrugged and grinned at the joke. "I was close by, and since I quit the ship, I just thought I'd go visit him and Mr. Gates."

Luke nodded as Jefferson continued.

"When he insisted on coming back up the river with me, I wasn't going to tell him no. They told us in Echuca where to find this place."

"You mean, they told *you*." Luke corrected him.

"That's right. What's the matter with people around here? They're carrying rifles around in the town, and everyone's acting nervous. No one would even *talk* to Luke. I don't remember it being like this."

Patrick and his sister exchanged a quick glance. So much had happened since Jefferson had left them several months ago. Not only had they found their father, but they had discovered their grandfather, as well. And now the trouble with the aborigines . . .

"It's our turn to tell *you* a story," said Becky, and they took turns telling Jefferson and Luke how the Old Man, the riverboat captain who had brought them to Echuca in search of John

McWaid, was really their grandfather—the same man who had been a prisoner with Gates so many years ago. Jefferson shook his head as if he couldn't believe what they were telling him.

"If that don't beat all," said Jefferson. "And now he's up trying to refloat the *Lady Elisabeth*? We were hopin' to catch a ride up the river with him."

Mrs. McWaid nodded, and a worried look crossed her face. "Last we heard from the captain, he said it was taking longer to raise the boat than he thought. I wouldn't let Patrick and Becky go with him, but now I'm starting to think *someone* should have. Just to keep him company."

"That's what I *told* you, Ma," said Patrick, but there was nothing to do about it. Not now.

"Of course, you two boys can stay here as long as you like," Mrs. McWaid told them as she looked around the small cabin. "I'm sure the captain wouldn't mind. We'll find a place for you to sleep."

"That would be just fine, ma'am," Jefferson smiled at Mrs. McWaid. "Only Luke here will probably insist on sleeping outside, the way he always has. Never one to stay inside. Slept out on the deck of the paddle steamer, even in the wind. Half crazy, if you ask—"

Suddenly, one of the glass windows in the pilothouse exploded just a few feet away from them.

"What's that?" cried Patrick, ducking down with his arms over his head. They heard another crash, this time like a rock against the side of the house. Glass flew in all directions, and Patrick felt something like a beesting on the cheek.

"Is everyone all right?" asked Jefferson, crouched down on the floor with everyone else.

Becky picked herself off the floor and brushed Michael off as she helped him stand. "Ma!" she exclaimed. "Your hair is full of glass!"

"Oh dear." Mrs. McWaid shook her head gently and then looked straight at Patrick. "Patrick, you've been cut on the face!"

Patrick put his hand to first one cheek, then the other. On the right cheek, Patrick felt blood. His stomach turned.

"A piece of glass caught you," said Jefferson. He reached over and picked up a smooth river rock about the size of a fist. "And someone's got a pretty good aim, I'd say."

Before anyone could say anything else, Jefferson ran for the door. Patrick was right behind him.

"Patrick, your cheek!" protested his mother.

Cheek or no cheek, they were out the door in a second, and Patrick scanned the riverfront for signs of anyone who would have thrown the rock. Jefferson pointed to a clearing between two over-hanging gum trees, then looked back at the broken window.

"Whoever it was probably stood right down there. You know who would do something like this?"

Patrick wasn't ready to explain about Sebastian and Will, not yet. He wished his father would make it back from town soon.

"It's a long story," he told Jefferson. "I'll tell you later. Let's keep looking."

They sprinted down to the riverbank. Luke joined them a moment later, his nose almost to the ground.

"Footprints!" he told them quietly.

In the gathering darkness Patrick couldn't quite see what the aborigine boy saw, but they followed him along the river toward Echuca. When Patrick finally paused to look down at himself, he could tell he was bleeding all over his shirt.

"Patrick, you look like you're dying with all that blood," Jefferson told him as they hurried along the riverbank. "You should go home and get that cleaned up."

"No pain," Patrick told him. "Really. It looks worse than it is."

"Hmm." Jefferson didn't seem so sure.

Luke said nothing, only concentrated on the ground as he led them on a weaving trail, stopping every so often. Finally he stood up straight and shook his head.

"It's too dark," he said. "We lost him. See all these tracks here? Horses, men, a couple of dingoes. They're all mixed together."

"Aborigines or white people?" asked Patrick, wiping his cheek once more.

Luke shook his head. "Can't tell. These tracks could be either. Why?"

As they trudged back to the cabin, Patrick told the boys a little about Sebastian and what had happened at the corroboree.

Jefferson whistled low, and Luke could only shake his head as if he didn't believe it all could be possible.

"And what did that Sebastian fellow say about aborigines again?" asked Luke, his eyebrows knit into a frown.

Seeing the look on Luke's face, Patrick wasn't sure how much he should repeat. "Said they weren't even smart enough to play a game like cricket."

Luke crossed his arms as they walked. "Maybe he'd prefer to play me in a game of chess."

Jefferson laughed. "He'd lose. I tried to beat Luke five times. Lost every one."

"The last one in only ten moves." A smile flashed across Luke's face for a moment before he turned serious once more.

"What do you think?" whispered Patrick.

"I think the same thing is happening now that happened to my parents," said Luke.

"Which is?"

"Settlers take from the aborigines, aborigines take it back, settlers go back with guns. . . ."

"Unless we do something," added Jefferson, "and soon."

The next afternoon after school Patrick was showing his friends the river, pointing out where the paddle steamers passed by and where the kookaburra birds sat in their trees hanging over the waters. But Jefferson wasn't listening. Without warning he hit his hands together.

"You know what we're going to do?" asked the American, not waiting for an answer. "We're going to march right over to that aborigine camp and find out for ourselves what's going on with this rustling thing. Those aborigine folks are in a load of trouble, and it looks like Patrick's right in the middle."

"I don't know if that's a good idea." Luke was straight-faced.

"You can translate for us, can't you?" Jefferson didn't slow down.

"Wrong." Luke held up his hand. "I'm Ngarrenderri, remember? My people came from the mouth of the river, not way up here. I think these are Yorta Yorta."

"And you don't understand the Yorta Yorta language?"

Luke sighed with impatience. "Maybe a few words here and there. No more than you probably understand German."

"Oh." Jefferson looked surprised. "I guess I just always assumed you were all—"

"All the same?" Luke finished the sentence with a chuckle. "There you go again, Yank. Different tribes speak different languages. I've tried to explain that to you, but you're a better chess player than you are a listener. And that's not very good."

"Well," suggested Patrick, "there's an older fellow there who spoke English pretty well. Maybe we'll find him again."

"Or maybe we can use sign language," said Jefferson. "How do you say, 'You've got to stop stealing horses from the white people'?"

By that time Michael had seen them walking and ran down to meet them. As usual, he was carrying his young koala. It had been growing the past several months and was almost too big for Michael to carry. His arms were scratched by the animal's long tree-climbing claws, but Michael never seemed to mind.

"Patrick!" Michael called out. "Did you ever catch the person who threw the rock?"

Patrick shook his head no.

"Pa went to get the constable. Ma was wondering where you were."

"Tell Ma we're fine. And tell her I'm just going—"

Patrick thought for a moment about Sebastian's warning, then put it out of his mind.

"I'm going to show Jefferson and Luke where the aborigine camp is."

"Can I come? I won't bring Christopher."

Patrick smiled and shook his head. "Not this time, Michael. You just go tell Ma where we're going and that we'll be back before dark."

Once they had rowed across the river and pulled their rowboat up on the shore, Patrick led his friends down a trail that skirted around the aborigine camp. He knew that this time there would be no festival music or campfire lights to guide him.

Halfway there Luke stiffened and they stopped. Patrick was about to open his mouth, but Luke stopped him with a stare.

"Did you hear that?" he whispered. Patrick strained his ears but couldn't tell what Luke was talking about.

"Birds?" he asked. Luke shook his head.

"I don't hear anything, either," said Jefferson. He began to take a step, but Luke grabbed him by the shoulder.

"There's someone behind us," warned Luke. "Don't turn around, and don't stare."

"What?" Jefferson did just what his friend told him not to do, then shrugged. "I think you're hearing things."

Patrick peeked behind them, but all he could see were trees leading down to the riverbank.

"Let's keep going," suggested Patrick, and they continued on.

"There's something else I didn't tell you." Luke finally looked nervously over his shoulder.

"You already told us you don't speak the language." Jefferson frowned.

"You don't understand." Luke shook his head. "There's more to it than that."

"What do you mean?" asked Patrick. He kept looking over his shoulder, too, but still he saw and heard nothing behind them.

"These aren't my people, remember." Luke pointed in the direction of the camp. "They might not appreciate me here."

"Really?" wondered Patrick. "What did you ever do to them?"

"It's not what I did." Luke shook his head. "It's who I am."

"Hmm." Jefferson scratched his head. "Kind of like a Yankee steppin' down the main street back home in Augusta, Arkansas."

Luke chuckled nervously. "Just a few years ago aborigines went to war if people from other tribes invaded their territory."

"Oh no," groaned Jefferson. "Why didn't you tell us that before?"

Luke sighed. "I thought it didn't matter anymore. And maybe it doesn't. Maybe I *am* just hearing things."

Suddenly, Patrick heard a noise in the bush behind them—footsteps coming their way. But before he could turn around he felt a sharp jab between the shoulder blades. Even without looking he knew an aborigine spear was pointed at his back.

CHAPTER 7

WELCOME TO DINGO CREEK

"Better try some of your language on them," suggested Jefferson. "There's a fellow with an Arkansas toothpick in my back, and I don't want him any closer. Tell him I'm an American."

"I'm sure he would be quite impressed," replied Luke, as stiff as the other two. No one dared look behind them, although Patrick could see Jefferson and Luke out of the corner of his eye.

"They might think we're your 'friends' from Echuca," whispered Jefferson, "back for more prisoners. At least they didn't throw their spears first and ask questions later."

Somewhere ahead of them Patrick heard shouting and thought he saw faces peeking out from behind trees. The spear holders grumbled behind them.

"Do you understand anything they're saying?" Patrick asked Luke.

"I told you before." Luke shook his head as they shuffled forward down the trail. "Only a word here and there. I'm not sure, except they want us to keep walking."

"I could tell you that much," put in Jefferson. "The one behind me is saying, 'How much will you give me if I string up this skinny one?'"

No one else laughed at Jefferson's joke.

At last they made it to the same clearing where Patrick had seen

61

the dance. This time, in the light, he could see shelters of leaves and bark hung over long, bent sticks and smoldering fire pits here and there.

"Where is everyone?" asked Patrick.

"Hello?" called Jefferson.

One of the men behind them hooted a warning, and a little boy stood up behind one of the shelters. Patrick could see stitches on his head.

"Hey there, Davey!" Patrick held up his hand when he recognized the boy, but the aborigine behind him batted his hand down with the side of his spear.

"Ow!" complained Patrick, and he finally turned to face his attacker with hands up. "Listen, I mean you no harm."

The spear holder wasn't much older than Patrick, probably Jefferson's age, and dressed like the rest of them in an odd assortment of worn clothes—a mixture of what looked like aborigine-style wraps and European clothes. He kept his sharp, metal-tipped spear pointed at Patrick but took a step backward when Davey cried out a few words Patrick couldn't understand.

After a moment of grumbling, the other two men lowered their spears, as well. Whatever he told the boy, it sounded as if he was disappointed.

"That's better," sighed Jefferson, turning around. "Well, boys, maybe this was not such a good idea after all, but here we are."

"I apologize for the way you were welcomed," said an old man from the edge of the clearing. The same old man Patrick had seen on the night of the dance tottered slowly toward them. Davey helped him sit down on a well-worn log. "But ever since the other night . . ."

The little boy whispered in the man's ear, as Patrick had seen him do before. He nodded and spoke softly back.

"Pardon me again, but my eyes don't work as well as they used to." He put his hand on his friend's shoulder. "So I borrow younger eyes. This is Davey. I think you've met."

Davey smiled at the sound of his name.

"You speak English very well." Jefferson looked amazed. "Are you the only one who does?"

"Others speak just a little. We prefer our own language. I'm not an English teacher.

"Your black friend speaks English, too," continued the man. Silver-haired and wrinkled like a raisin, he turned his head up and to the side as he spoke, as if using his ears to locate them. "But he's not Yorta Yorta."

"No," Luke finally spoke up. "I'm from the Ngarrenderri, near the mouth of the river."

The silver-haired man's eyebrows shot up, as if that was important news. He spoke to the tribe, and Patrick could only hear the word "Ngarrenderri."

One of the young men of the tribe cautiously stepped up behind Luke and pulled at the back of his shirt.

"Watch out, Luke," warned Jefferson, and Luke whirled around to face the curious aborigine, who backed up with a scowl.

"I think he wants to see your back," guessed the older man. "He wants to see your scars."

Scars? wondered Patrick, but Luke only nodded and pulled up the back of his shirt for the others to see. Patrick noticed an ugly scar across Luke's side, a jagged stripe about four inches long. A couple of aborigines looked closer, sniffed, and laughed.

"Not very big, they say." The silver-haired man grunted with amusement. "Your tribe's not as fierce as they thought."

"Tell them I wasn't raised in a tribe," replied Luke.

Patrick looked at his friend in confusion. "What are they talking about?" he whispered.

"When boys become men, they're cut in a special ceremony," Luke whispered back. "The scars show which tribe you come from. The scars show you're a man."

Patrick made a face at the grisly thought. "But how did *you* get your scar?"

Luke smiled and lowered his voice. "Fell against the end of a metal railing at the lighthouse when I was six. Got infected for a while. Want to see another?"

Patrick shook his head but smiled along with his friend.

"They're impressed, Luke," said Jefferson. "Let me try this."

Jefferson puffed out his chest, raised his voice, and nearly shouted at the old man. "I'm from the American South," he hollered. "Arkansas. Augusta, Arkansas. I've got a couple of scars, too. One here on my thumb, see?"

His announcement brought blank stares.

"Arkansas?" repeated a younger boy, coming closer and poking Jefferson in the side.

"I don't think your scars measure up, Jeff," suggested Patrick.

Jefferson looked miffed, but Patrick had to grin. The silver-haired man spoke up once more.

"My name is Moses, Mr. Arkansas. That was the name they gave me on the cattle station I worked when I was a boy, where I learned your language. But then I became ill and lost my eyesight, so I came back to my people. Things are very different now, aren't they? Even people who can see, they don't always see things very clearly."

None of them knew what to say, so they listened to the wrinkled man as he told them about his people and the hard times they lived in. Once Patrick got used to the odd accent, he could understand just fine. The man actually sounded a lot like Luke. Patrick was curious how old he was.

As old as Grandpa? he wondered.

"But you didn't come to hear me tell you about our troubles." After a while the aborigine leader crossed his arms and stared absently into the darkening sky. "Why *are* you here now?"

Patrick looked around at the dark-skinned people who had crowded around to see. Some of the women wore opossum-skin blankets around their shoulders, while others had English-style dresses. One man had on a headband with a large, single emu feather tucked in the side. Some carried long wooden spears, others large boomerangs.

Luke jabbed Jefferson with his elbow. "You tell him why we came. It was your idea."

Patrick tried not to think of what might happen if Sebastian or Will discovered they had visited the aborigines again.

"We heard about all the horse stealing going on around Echuca," began Jefferson. "And my friend Patrick here got himself in the middle of this fight between y'all and those characters in town. We wanted to find out for ourselves about the two aborigines in jail for stealing—"

Jefferson couldn't finish what he was saying over all the shouts that suddenly met his translated words. Even Moses scowled at them.

This does not sound friendly, decided Patrick. He looked behind him for the boys with the spears.

"Now you've done it, Jeff," Luke yelled at them. "I think we'd better leave."

But there was no escaping the shouting aborigines who pressed in on them from all sides. One of the children stepped up and hit Jefferson in the back with his fist, and Patrick wheeled around to defend himself.

"He meant no harm," Patrick shouted to Moses.

Moses raised his hands and his voice so that gradually the shouting settled down, but the people still didn't back away from Patrick, Luke, and Jefferson.

"Next time you'd better let me do the talking," whispered Luke.

"You know I would have let you," Jefferson shot back.

An older boy stared at Jeff, spear in hand.

And he looks quite ready to use it, worried Patrick.

"We didn't come here to make trouble," Patrick finally said. "Is there some way we can help you?"

After the words were translated, the young aborigine with the spear and the stare blurted out some instructions. He never took his eyes off Patrick, never eased his grip on the spear.

"He says you can help them rescue their brothers from the jail," said Moses. "And then there will be revenge."

Patrick closed his eyes and groaned quietly.

"This is worse than I thought," said Luke.

"I think it's really time to skedaddle," muttered Jefferson.

"Listen to me." Patrick put up his hands. He prayed silently, not knowing what words could calm the riot that had broken out around them. A couple of men waved their hands in disgust, but most of them fell silent as Davey spoke up.

"The little one said to let you speak," said Moses. "Now, what will you say?"

What will I say, Lord? Patrick prayed quietly and swallowed hard. He looked at the black eyes that followed each move he made, and a shiver went up his spine. He didn't want to know what they might do with their spears.

"My father, John McWaid was put in jail once, too," Patrick began, "even though he had done nothing wrong."

He talked slowly, letting Moses change the words into Yorta Yorta.

So far, so good. Patrick looked around at his audience. *They're nodding*.

"But we found out the truth, and the English had to set him free."

"Preach it," whispered Jefferson.

"Now, I don't know why you're stealing settlers' horses, but—" A couple of men scowled at the words, but Patrick took a deep breath and continued. "But we're not like the bullies from town. We want to be fair and listen to your story, not rush to say you did this or that. Why, those bullies even said they didn't think you could play an English game like cricket, and we know that's not true."

The scowls turned back to smiles.

"What I'm trying to say is, maybe we can help *you*."

Patrick could hardly believe the words that had just escaped his mouth, but it was too late. His audience cheered as Moses translated the last part. Even the men holding their spears grinned.

"How are you going to help us?" asked Moses.

"Uh . . ." Patrick felt his jaw drop. He had said far more than he intended to. "Maybe I didn't mean to say that last part."

A parrot of some kind screeched in the eucalyptus branches far above. A man in the background asked a question, and Moses stroked his beard.

"He wants to know when we're going to learn this cricket game. You'll teach us."

"Pardon?" asked Jefferson. "I don't think that's what Patrick meant to—"

"But you know this English game, Mr. Patrick?" interrupted Moses. "Don't you?"

"Well, a little," admitted Patrick, afraid he wouldn't look as smart as he had talked. "I know just a little."

"That is enough." Moses smiled. "You will teach us how to play cricket. It's only right, as you say, since aborigines helped your father when he lived in the bush. You do this for us."

"We'll do it," agreed Luke, too quickly for Patrick's comfort.

"Wait a minute. I can't . . ." began Patrick, then he looked at the fellow with the spear and sighed. He wasn't sure how Moses knew about his father, but he supposed word had gotten around. *What have I gotten myself into?*

Jefferson threw up his hands. "Don't look at me. I'm an American, remember? We don't play English games in Arkansas. Maybe in Philadelphia, but not in *my* town."

"You play baseball, don't you?" Luke turned to him. Patrick wondered how the aborigine boy knew about the American game.

"Well, sure." Jefferson wrinkled his forehead. "Everyone knows how to play baseball. It's the latest—"

"Baseball has a ball and a bat, right?" Luke continued to press the point.

"Yes, but—"

"You hit the ball with the bat and you run, don't you?"

Jefferson nodded. Luke smiled and put up his hands to make his point.

"So you can show them what you know."

Jefferson crossed his arms. "How do *you* know so much about the game?"

Luke shrugged his shoulders and smiled.

"Fine!" Moses clapped his hands. "The Ngarrenderri knows cricket, too! We'll learn this game tomorrow. And we'll beat the English. Revenge."

"Revenge?" Patrick bit his lip. "No, wait. I don't know—"

"Cricket won't get your friends out of jail, understand." Luke put up his hand.

By that time it was too late. Everyone in the camp cheered, and Davey shyly handed Patrick a plate made from a piece of bark. He pointed at what looked like a piece of white meat, then pointed to his mouth.

"He wants you to eat it," Luke told him, and he smiled. Patrick sniffed the food carefully, trying not to look rude.

"Go on." Jefferson grinned. "You got yourself into this."

"Easy for you to say," Patrick whispered back, but he held the meat between his fingers—for he was pretty sure it was meat—and downed it in one swallow.

"You like it?" asked Moses. "Snake meat. A delicacy."

"Great." Patrick felt his stomach do a flip as he clenched his teeth, even though it didn't taste that bad.

Moses smiled, showing a few crooked, yellow teeth, while the rest of the tribe finally pulled back to let Patrick, Luke, and Jefferson back out the way they came.

"You'll be back, then." Moses settled himself by the fire and helped himself to a long, charred black onion. He peeled back the outer leaves, tossed them to the ground, and sucked on the shoot in the middle. His words were a command.

"Tomorrow," promised Luke.

When they were far enough away, all three broke into a run, crashing through the bush to make it back to the rowboat.

"Why in the world did you tell them we knew about cricket?" asked Patrick, struggling to keep up with the other two. "I thought we were just going there to find out a little more about the stolen horses."

Luke grinned as he pulled ahead of the race. "I thought you preached a wonderful sermon."

"You don't understand." Patrick gritted his teeth and pumped his arms, but Luke was too fast for either of them. "I don't know anything about cricket."

"That's not what you said back there," answered Luke.

If Sebastian finds out . . . But Patrick didn't dare say what he thought.

By that time Luke had made it to the riverbank, where he stood looking. Jefferson and Patrick nearly ran into him, and they stood on the spot where they had pulled up their boat. With his eyes Patrick followed a line through the mud where the boat had been dragged down to the water, and then . . .

"I can't believe it," whispered Luke. "It's gone."

CHAPTER 8

RUNNING AWAY

They tried to search the mud for clues, but it was only a jumble of footprints.

"Do you think some of those aborigines came and sailed it down the river?" wondered Patrick out loud.

They stood for a moment, searching the river. The early evening sky reflected a deep bluish-purple on the water as it rippled between the twin reflections of red river gum trees leaning toward the Murray on either side.

"Gone," echoed Jefferson, slapping his fist. "But I know I tied it up to that tree branch with two half hitches."

Patrick nodded his head. "Sure enough you did. But look over there on the other side of the river."

"Where?" asked Jefferson, staring out in the direction Patrick indicated.

Luke slipped down the muddy bank and waded into the water up to his knees. He pointed down the river at an overhanging branch.

"I see it, too. It's down there—on the other side."

"I thought we pulled it up high enough not to wash down the river," grumbled Jefferson. "Water's too cold to go swimming."

"I don't know who took it," said Luke, "but I'll race you to the other side."

Patrick took up the challenge, peeling off his shirt and plunging into the water. When it hit his chest like a thousand needles, it nearly took his breath away.

"Woo!" he whooped, taking a few strokes to fight off the bitter, numbing cold. He turned over on his back and checked on Jefferson, who was still pacing on the bank with his hands on his hips.

"Come on, Jeff!" he called out. "Water's fine!"

Jefferson just frowned. "You know what kind of swimmer I am."

"All right, fine. We'll be back with the boat in just a minute."

But it was farther to the other side than it looked from the shore, and before Patrick knew it, his arms had turned to dead weight and a bolt of sudden pain shot through the back of his leg at the calf.

"Luke!" gasped Patrick. "I got a cramp in my leg!"

The cramp doubled him over in pain, and he gripped the back of his leg as the current drifted him under the water and downriver. Instantly helpless, he swallowed a gallon of river water, choked, and reached up desperately for help.

Luke had crawled up on the far bank and glanced at Patrick in surprise. But Patrick could only wave weakly and hope that Luke could see he wasn't kidding. Luke stood by their swamped boat where it had wedged against a snag of branches.

"Patrick?" he asked. Without waiting for an answer, he grabbed one end of the rowboat and shoved it back into the river. It only half floated, but that was enough. A moment later Patrick felt himself yanked roughly over the side of the boat.

Patrick coughed as the boat turned turtle. The current caught and twirled the upside-down boat into the middle of the chocolate river, but at least he had something to hang on to.

"Where are you going?" yelled Jefferson from the other side as he watched them drift farther way. "I'm up here!"

"Are you all right?" asked Luke, and Patrick nodded weakly. The pain still crippled his right leg, but he wasn't going to drown. While Patrick used his hand to paddle as best he could, Luke kicked strongly from the rear so they made a slow, zigzag course across to Jefferson's side.

"What happened to y'all?" asked Jefferson as he pulled them in. Patrick staggered to safety and lay panting alongside the boat.

"Patrick got a cramp in his leg," explained Luke.

"Oh" was all Jefferson said.

Patrick shook his head to clear it, and the other two righted the boat and poured out all the water. All three had to paddle with their hands to get back across.

In the middle of the river, though, Jefferson nearly tipped the boat over when he stood up and started waving.

"Hey, there!" he cried. "Becky!"

Drifting down the river, the boys noticed Becky standing by a gnarled stump at the edge of the water. She was waving back at them almost as hard as Jefferson waved at her. She straightened her blue-checked dress and waited for them to land.

"Interesting way to cross over," she told them, grabbing at Jefferson's hand to pull them in. "What were you doing over there?"

Luke cleared his throat.

Jefferson studied his muddy shoes.

"Uh . . ." Patrick wondered if their explanation would sound silly. "Jeff and Luke were arranging for a cricket match."

Becky laughed as if it were a joke.

"Actually, we thought we'd just take a dip," he told her as they carried the boat back up toward the cabin.

"In the middle of winter? You're daft. Completely crazy."

"Jeff thought it would be a good idea to go talk with the aborigines," explained Patrick. "While we were over there, someone cut our boat loose."

"Hmm." Becky frowned. "I don't know why anyone would do that."

"Same reason why someone threw a rock through our window."

"Well, now that you mention him, let me tell you what I've been thinking."

"They don't want to hear it, Becky—" began Patrick. He thought back to his run-in with Sebastian and Will the day before. He remembered the threats, the threats no one else knew about.

"Sure we do," said Jefferson, giving Becky a hand as they climbed up the bank.

"I think there is something very, very odd about this situation with the aborigines." Becky slapped her hands together after they had safely tied the boat to a willow tree. "And I think—"

"Becky," Patrick interrupted and held up his hand. "I really don't think it's a good idea for you to be investigating this anymore."

"What?" Becky stopped to look at her brother. "What are you talking about?"

"Just what I said. I think we should leave it to the constable. It could be dangerous."

"I'm fifteen years old, Patrick McWaid. And besides, I don't think the constable is at all interested in finding out what really happened."

"You don't understand."

"No? Explain it to me, then, will you?" Becky's fine lips turned down in an angry pout.

"I can't." Patrick sighed as they turned a corner in the short path from the river, then stopped short of the cabin.

The constable!

Constable Fitzgerald stood by the front door of their cabin, talking to their father. When he turned toward them, he wore a scowl on his face.

"G'day." The constable waited for Patrick and the others to walk up to the cabin. "Heard there was trouble out here."

It took only a moment to realize the constable was talking about the broken glass incident.

"We followed the tracks," said Patrick, "but it was a dead end."

"That so?" Constable Fitzgerald eyed Luke carefully but didn't ask any more questions as he walked around their cabin to see where the broken glass had fallen.

"And you didn't see anyone?" The constable picked up a shard of jagged glass.

Patrick looked at the others and shook his head. Constable Fitzgerald turned back to Patrick's parents.

"I'll have my assistant look into it," he told them, striding back to his horse and climbing up. "This sort of thing happens. You live pretty close to those aborigines over there."

"Wait, Alexander," said Patrick's father.

The constable didn't seem to hear. "Keep your children out of trouble, John. And out of the river, for that matter. Feel free to look me up again if it's anything *serious.*" With that he turned away and spurred his black horse to a gallop. Everyone stared quietly at the constable as he disappeared down the trail.

"The constable's a good man," their father told them. He had returned to picking out broken glass from the window frame. "But you know he's busy. I suppose he has bigger things to worry about than a broken window."

"Obviously," sighed their mother, turning to go back inside. She gave Patrick a curious look, just as the constable had done, while Luke and Jeff hurried off toward the woodpile.

"Patrick, are you going to explain what happened to you?" asked Mr. McWaid.

"Boys and boats," answered Becky, as if that explained everything, and she followed her mother into the cabin.

Patrick looked again down the lane, then back at his father still picking glass out of the window frame. He crossed his arms and kicked at the ground.

"I assume there's a good reason for your being wet," said Mr. McWaid.

"Someone took our boat back across the river."

"I see. So you—"

"We swam back across." Patrick finished the sentence, leaving out the part about his leg cramp.

"Hmm." His father nodded and went back to his work.

Patrick looked out into the early evening and thought about Sebastian and Will. Sebastian with his club, beating him silly, or even the horse thief aborigines with their wicked spears. He couldn't decide which was worse. All he knew was that he could think of nothing else ever since he had run across the aborigines in the bush that night.

"Pa, what would happen if we just went back to Dublin?"

"We've discussed this before, son."

"I know it's a lot of money for passage," continued Patrick. "But now that you're out of prison, and since things were cleared up back home, you could get your old job back, couldn't you?"

"It's not that easy, son."

"Isn't your job here just temporary?"

"We think this might be a good place to settle. Your mother and I have been praying about it."

"What's to pray about?" Patrick picked up a piece of glass. "People hate us here."

"Is that what this is all about?" asked Mr. McWaid. "I thought you liked being close to your grandfather and all."

"Sure, when he's here. But he's always on the river."

"Who hates you, then?"

Patrick couldn't answer. He shivered in his damp clothes.

"We couldn't leave Christopher," put in Michael, and Patrick turned to see his little brother listening from just inside the house. As usual, Michael had picked up his koala to feed the cuddly animal a handful of gum tree leaves.

"This has nothing to do with your koala." Patrick turned to his brother. "And you stay out of this. I was talking to Pa."

"But Christopher's part of this family, too!" insisted Michael, stroking his koala. "And besides, I like it here. I don't want to move."

"Are we talking about moving again?" Becky joined in the conversation from inside the cabin.

"I was just trying to ask Pa a question," replied Patrick, feeling his voice raise a notch. "Now everyone is against me."

"No one's against you, Patrick." Mr. McWaid started to put his arm around his son, but Patrick stepped back. "But is there anything else that'd be bothering you?"

"No!" Patrick almost shouted. "Nothing else. I just wanted to know when we could move back home and get away from . . ." His voice trailed off when he realized what he was saying.

"There's someone you want to get away from?" His father

wanted to know. "Would that be what we're discussing here?"

"This place . . ." Patrick tried once more to explain, but he couldn't. This place that he loved and hated all at the same time.

"Echuca seems like a good place for our family," continued their father. "The teacher at school is good—"

"Pretty good," interrupted Patrick.

His father ignored the comment and continued. "The people at church are friendly, and now that I've started this new job—"

"We're not leaving, are we?" wailed Michael, holding his koala more tightly. Christopher stared at them with his enormous black eyes.

"Hush. No." Their mother stepped up and patted Michael on the arm. "No one is going anywhere. Not now, at least."

"But, Ma, you were sad to leave Dublin," Patrick tried once again. "I know you were."

Their mother crossed her arms. "Well, yes, of course I was, but now—"

"Don't you all understand?" shouted Patrick. "People hate us here. We've got to get away. We've got to go back home."

How can I make them understand?

"Patrick," said his mother in a softer voice, "why don't you lower your voice, come in here, and dry off?"

"I'm quite dry now," replied Patrick. His wet shoe made a squishing sound as he ran away from the cabin past Luke and Jefferson, who were just bringing in armloads of wood for Mrs. McWaid's stove.

"What's wrong with him?" asked Jefferson.

Patrick just kept running, trying to forget everything they had talked about. But even the bullfrogs reminded him as he stood on the riverbank, staring at the dark water flowing past. On the other side, a small tree moved.

"What's that?" Patrick almost blurted out as he pulled behind a gum tree. The shape was nearly as dark as the evening sky, and all Patrick was sure of was that it was an aborigine. Certainly not Luke. But the person, whoever he was, just eyed Patrick silently in the early evening light.

Another horse thief? Patrick wondered.

As they studied each other, no one moved for what seemed like an eternity. Finally the dark figure gripped and shook his spear in front of his chest, like a warning, a dare for Patrick to cross over again. Even without words, the meaning was clear: "Cross over here, boy, and you'll find trouble."

Patrick shivered—not just from the cold—and held his position behind the gum tree. The aborigine pulled back silently into the bush, as if daring Patrick to follow.

CHAPTER 9

Arkansas Cricket

"Come on," said Jefferson, sitting at the oars of the rowboat the next afternoon. Luke was in the front of the boat, trying not to tip it over. "We're waiting for you. Push us off and get in, will you?"

"You two go on without me." Patrick scanned the far shore and bit his lip.

"Sakes alive! What's wrong with you?" asked Jefferson. He leaned over and grabbed Patrick's wrist. "Last night you're homesick, and today you're afraid to cross the river. You're acting like a crazy coot."

Like a what? Patrick yanked his wrist away and gave the boat a shove with his foot.

"You're not coming?" asked Luke. His eyes squinted in a question mark as the current caught the boat and it began to drift away. Patrick hesitated.

"I'm coming." Patrick waded into the ankle-deep water and jumped into the back of the boat. "And I'm no coot, or whatever it was you called me."

Jefferson chuckled as he began rowing. Patrick kept a worried eye out for the aborigine with the spear. So far, so good.

"I don't know what you're worried about," Jefferson said as they beached the boat a few minutes later. Patrick didn't answer, just kept looking for anyone who might be hiding in the bush. He half expected a shout or a spear to come flying through the air.

"Patrick?" Luke looked at him again.

"I'm fine." Patrick waved his hand and followed them up the trail toward Dingo Creek and the aborigine camp. "I'm sorry. I was just thinking."

Jefferson raised his eyebrows. "Oh, the coot is thinking now, is he?"

Patrick was silent for a few minutes, but he couldn't stop his mind from racing.

"How do we even know the fellows in town will agree to play the aborigine team?" he finally whispered.

"They'll play." Jefferson crossed his arms as he walked ahead of the two other boys. "It'll be a challenge. They won't walk away from a challenge. Especially not this one."

"You don't know them," Patrick countered.

Jefferson shrugged. "I know their type."

Luke chuckled at the comment.

"The real challenge," continued Patrick, "is going to be teaching the aborigines a game we don't know how to play."

Luke grinned. "I've played cricket before."

"Really?" Patrick had a hard time imagining the aborigine boy, raised on an island at a remote lighthouse, playing an English gentleman's sport.

"Gates taught me how," continued Luke. "There was even a team in Kingscoate . . . well, sort of a team. I played a few times. And I've read books. . . ."

"Ask him anything," Jefferson pointed his thumb at Luke with a smile, "and he's read a book on the subject. I've never met a body who's read more."

"But there's a lot more to the game than just bowling and hitting." Patrick tried to recall everything he could about the game from the few times he had seen it played. "There are eleven men on a side, I think, against two fellows who take turns hitting the ball. And an oval playing field, and the two wickets . . ."

"Gates taught me all that, too," Luke assured them with an easy wave of his hand.

"Well, I'm glad *someone* knows this game." Jefferson scratched his head. "Because all I'm going to be able to tell you is how to swing a bat and how to hit a home run."

"There aren't any home runs in cricket," explained Luke. "They have singles, fours, and sixes."

"Right." Jefferson nodded. "So I'll show them how to pitch the ball."

"No, no," Luke corrected him. "You don't pitch, you bowl. Keep your arm straight when you go through the swing. Then you bounce the ball right in front of the batsman."

As they walked toward Dingo Creek, Luke went through the motions a couple times to show Jeff what he was talking about. Patrick couldn't keep from imagining the spear-thrower hiding behind the next tree, and he hung back.

"Well, how about base running?" concluded Jefferson. "Can I show them that?"

"That might be hard." Luke flashed a smile. "There aren't any bases in cricket, and two players run at the same time."

"Oh." Jefferson scratched his head. "This is going to be a great game for an Arkansas farm boy. We're going to need your help, Patrick."

"This is your thing. I'm just going to watch." Patrick looked around once more and shook his head. He jumped when he saw several dark figures sprinting their direction. But instead of the aborigine with the spear, they were greeted by a waving, smiling mob of children. They all shouted a cheer in their language.

"What are they all saying?" asked Patrick.

The kids giggled and kept repeating their song, and the words almost reminded Patrick of the way the Murray flowed and snaked its way past their cabin. What was the word he heard over and over? As they sang, the children grabbed his hands and dragged them to the camp.

"Sounds like 'Arkansaw Cricket' to me," Patrick finally guessed.

Jefferson laughed. "That's it, all right."

"We're here, Mister Moses." Luke looked around the camp as he called out, but the aborigine leader already stood waiting for them, his young guide at his side. Moses motioned for them to follow him out the other side of the camp. The people just stared and whispered.

"It's the Arkansas Cricket and his two friends," said Luke quietly.

Patrick was nervous, but he had to giggle at the crazy situation he was in. When they arrived at a clearing, they found a group of about ten or eleven boys in their teens. Some were as young as Patrick, but most looked like they were fifteen or sixteen years old.

Jefferson looked around at the group and nodded. "So this is the team?"

Moses stood off to the side, like a proud father. "This is your team," he announced, holding up his hand and adding a few words in his own language. The aborigine boys all smiled and cheered, except for one, who stood off to the side and scowled. Patrick felt a shiver run up his spine when he recognized the aborigine, the same one who had waved the spear at him the night before.

"Who's that?" he whispered to the aborigine leader, forgetting for just a moment that Moses was blind.

"The unhappy one off to the side?" asked the silver-haired leader. "His name is Matthew."

This man sees as much as we do! thought Patrick.

"He's angry at the world, so you'd best stay out of his way," continued Moses. Patrick thought to himself that he probably wouldn't have any trouble doing that. "But he throws the spear better than anyone else on your new team. He'll be able to play this cricket game of yours. So explain it."

Patrick nodded. "I'll stay out of his way."

Moses listened to the rest of the group, then shouted back. Everyone stopped chattering and faced them.

"What did you say?" asked Jefferson, standing in the middle of the crowd.

Moses cleared his throat. "I just told them to listen to the Irish now. He is the game leader. You tell me how to play the game, and I will tell them. Go on."

"No, no, you don't understand. I'm just going to watch." Patrick looked first at Moses, staring up at the sky, then at the dark eyes focused on him. A couple held spears, including Matthew. Luke grinned and stepped forward to rescue him.

"First," Luke began, "let me tell you that the English game has many laws."

Moses followed with a burst of the aborigine language, and the team nodded.

"We'll need to practice many times before we're ready to play."

The team grumbled and looked even less pleased than they already were.

"We'll need a ball, and we'll need a couple of bats. We'll carve them from tree branches."

The children watched every move they made. Several ran off to get sticks.

"I hope they don't think that if they win a cricket match," Patrick whispered to Jefferson, "they'll get their friends out of jail."

"They're not like that, Patrick." Luke looked offended. "They know what they've asked us to do. They want to prove they can win the English game. That we're just as good . . . I mean, that *they're* just as good as the English."

"But if they know so much," replied Patrick, "why did those two aborigine fellows try to steal horses?"

"Shh," Jefferson warned him with a look at the spear-thrower, and Patrick said no more.

Luke's first job was to explain the game. With Jefferson's help he scratched out a map of where the eleven fielders on the one team and two batsmen on the other team would stand and play in a real match.

"The field is an oval, like this," began Luke.

I know that much about the game, Patrick told himself, standing back at a distance. Luke stepped forward, scratching a mark in the dirt where each player would stand.

"A long circle," explained Luke. "One of the eleven throws the ball, bowls it underhanded, toward one of the two batsmen. He tries to knock over the wooden pieces balanced on the two or three sticks. The batsman tries to keep him from hitting the sticks and hits the ball away instead. But if he can hit the ball far enough away from the fielders so he can run to the other end while his partner runs to his end . . ."

Most of the boys looked at the aborigine boy with confused stares, but Luke just continued.

"Then his team gets what we used to call notches, because they would carve notches in a stick for each run. Notches. Runs. Same thing."

Even Patrick was wondering if he could keep up with Luke's explanation, but Moses managed to keep translating everything into their language.

"Then when the batsman hits the ball"—Luke swung a stick and drew a few lines in the dirt—"the two batsmen switch places quickly, running back and forth to get runs, before a player on the fielding side—one of the ten fielders—throws the ball back to the wicket keeper. The team with the most runs wins."

At the edge of the clearing, Matthew leaned against a gum tree, his arms crossed stubbornly. His spear was at his side, and Patrick tried not to look at him.

"Does he understand what we're saying?" Jefferson finally asked. "That fellow Matthew over there. Does he understand the part about throwing the ball?"

When he heard the question repeated to him, Matthew straightened up and aimed his spear straight at Jefferson and Patrick. With a yell they both dropped to the ground as the spear whistled over their heads. Patrick looked up to see the spear still quivering, its tip buried in the gnarled side of an old gum tree.

"Matthew!" shouted Moses, hearing what had happened, but Matthew only stalked off after shouting a few more angry-sounding words at the group.

"What did he say?" asked Jefferson, getting to his knees. Moses was still scolding the boy, who had disappeared into the bush.

Moses shook his head. "He's impatient. He wants to know how the game is going to bring back our people from the English jail. I told him that first we have to show the English we can beat them at their game. That will be our revenge."

Patrick felt a knot inside his stomach at the words, but he took a deep breath and nodded.

And if the aborigines don't win? he wondered. *What will Matthew do then?*

"Go on ahead," Jefferson had told him when they were almost back to the cabin. "I'm going to see where Luke went. And your ma said she would be at the neighbors'."

"Right. The Duggans." Patrick nodded absently. "Jack Duggan's been working on his cousin's paddle steamer. He's about your age. I think you'd like him."

"Hmm," replied Jeff, stepping aside to wander along the river-bank on his own. "Could be."

"Helped us quite a bit a few months ago while you were gone. He found us when we were lost in the bush. He's a pretty decent fellow."

Jefferson nodded and walked away, down along the river, and Patrick let his mind wander back to Dingo Creek and the time they had spent with the all-aborigine team.

One thing is sure, he told himself. *The boys have talent. Natural talent. Or maybe they're just used to throwing so many spears and boomerangs.*

It was true. Most of the aborigine boys could throw the ball and hit the wooden wicket poles Luke had set up, even from far across the clearing. A few of them could bat the heavy string-wrapped ball Luke had brought along. In fact, they could hit it so far that they had almost lost the ball in the first ten minutes of practice.

"Just teach them the rules," Luke had said back at Dingo Creek, "and there will be no team they can't beat."

Maybe he's right, thought Patrick, climbing the last rise to their dark cabin alone, leaving Luke and Jeff by the river. Pa would still be working at the newspaper, and Ma, Becky, and Michael were at the Duggans'. *I'll have to light a lantern soon . . .*

His thoughts were interrupted by the sound of a horse, then shattering glass and a laugh.

CHAPTER 10

THE CHALLENGE

What? Patrick started to run toward the cabin. *Not again!*

More glass shattered, then Patrick heard a muffled shout that sounded like "Come on!"

"Hey!" shouted Patrick without thinking. He turned the corner and stood face-to-face with the tall, dark figure of Sebastian Weatherby.

"Hey, Will!" Sebastian shouted at his friend, seated on his black horse. "Look who's here."

Patrick stood still for a moment, the words frozen in his throat. Part of him wanted to turn and run.

"We, ah, heard a window breaking," began Sebastian, grinning at his friend. "Right, Will?"

"Sure," agreed the older boy on the horse. Will dropped a fist-sized stone behind him. "That's right. We came to see what was going on."

"Do you think I'm stupid?" blurted out Patrick. *When are Jefferson and Luke going to get here?*

"Only if you don't get the warning." Sebastian sneered and jerked his thumb at the cabin, where another window was broken out. That one, plus the two that had already been shattered.

"We never did anything to you." Patrick looked over his shoulder, hoping to see Jefferson walking up the trail from the river.

86

"No?" Sebastian caught him by the shoulder and whirled him around. At the same time, Will shoved Patrick square in the back with his boot. The next thing Patrick knew, he was face-down in the dirt and Sebastian was sitting on top of him.

Patrick gasped for air, but the older boy only pushed his face down harder.

"Can you count to three?" demanded Sebastian.

I could if you'd let me get my nose out of the dirt, thought Patrick, but he didn't answer.

"One, your sister's still asking questions around town. I already warned you about what's going to happen to her."

Patrick squirmed and grunted, struggling for air.

"Two, now you're keeping company with an aborigine kid, and—"

"You have a problem with that?" Patrick gasped, raising his chin.

Sebastian laughed. "He speaks."

Patrick tried to clear his throat and spit the gravel out of his mouth.

"Your dark friend is just like your sister, Irish boy. He's going to be very sorry—"

"If he doesn't go back to his own people," finished Will.

"That's right," laughed Sebastian. He pressed down even harder, flattening Patrick's cheek to the ground. "And just one more thing. You're spending a lot of time with the aborigines yourself, aren't you?"

"Why do you care?"

"Never mind. Just tell me what you're doing teaching those aborigines a gentleman's game. I thought I warned you not to go near them."

He's been spying on us, realized Patrick.

"Well?" Sebastian shifted his weight, but Patrick still could hardly breathe.

"They're challenging the new town team to a match," Patrick blurted out, which only set Sebastian and Will to laughing. At last the bigger boy rolled off Patrick's back as he howled and snorted.

"Did you hear him?" Sebastian took a deep breath before launching into another fit of laughing. "I thought he said the darkies wanted to play us in cricket."

"That's what I said." Patrick scrambled to his feet when he got the chance. "And they'll beat you, too."

Sebastian dismissed him as if he were a bug in front of his face. "You and those horse-thieving aborigines couldn't beat us if your lives depended on it. I told you before they wouldn't even be able to understand the rules."

"You'll be surprised," Patrick blurted out.

Sebastian ignored the comment. "We've got a couple of fellows who used to play on the best teams in England."

"If we *did* win, though," Patrick argued, "would you leave me and my sister alone?"

"Oh, absolutely." Sebastian put on a pretend serious face and solemnly raised his right hand, as if he were in a courtroom. "If you and your dark friends can beat my team, we'll be your servants for the rest of our natural born days. Right, Will?"

"For certain." Will laughed. "But there's not a chance of that."

"You'll stop bothering the aborigines?" Patrick didn't trust the older boy for a minute, but he at least wanted to hear it.

"Sure." Sebastian grabbed Patrick by the throat and stared straight into his eyes, and Patrick knew better than to duck away. "But when *we* win, you and your ignorant sister are going to do the same for us. You're going to leave Will's poor aunt alone and stay out of business that's not yours."

Patrick felt his head nodding.

"Is that your word?" demanded Sebastian, his face only inches from Patrick's.

What else can I say? Patrick's mind raced, and when he nodded again Sebastian grinned and threw him to the ground.

"Let's go, Will. He's a man of his word."

Sebastian climbed up behind Will on the back of the horse, and the black mare seemed to stagger for a moment under the weight. Will pulled his horse around in a circle with a vicious yank on the reins, nearly trampling Patrick in the process.

"A week from Saturday, then," Sebastian sneered. "We'll give you a few more days to practice up."

"Yeh," grinned Will. "You're going to need it."

Sebastian laughed as their horse trotted back down the lane. Patrick could only stare, his hands clenched into fists at his sides.

"Oh, and I hope you find the codfish who broke your windows." Sebastian looked back over his shoulder. "We'll keep an eye out. Maybe it's the same troublemakers who untied your boat."

Will chuckled and the two were gone.

Now what have I done? Patrick asked himself.

"I still can't believe you said we'd play them so soon." Jefferson rested a homemade cricket bat on his shoulder the next afternoon at their regular practice, after Patrick and Becky had returned from town. Next to him, one of the aborigine boys from the Dingo Creek camp was trying to imitate Jeff's swing.

"I wish you'd asked us first," said Luke, tossing the leather-covered hardball to another player. "We need more time than that to get ready. At least another month or two."

"I'm sorry." Patrick kicked at the ground. "They didn't ask— they just told me. I really didn't have a choice."

Moses sat at the edge of the clearing in his usual spot on a fallen tree and listened to the conversation. He smiled as soon as he heard Patrick's news about the match-up between the aborigines and the town team. "At least the boys will be happy for a chance to play."

Patrick frowned and looked down at his feet. "No. I should never have said anything. Things just come out of my mouth sometimes, and I say things I shouldn't. I'm sorry."

"Well." Luke tossed the ball to the aborigine boy who was playing wicket keeper behind the batsman and the three sticks called the wicket. "This was what we wanted to do, wasn't it? Play the town team? It's just happening a little sooner than we expected."

"We don't want to just *play* the town team," said Jefferson. "We want to *beat* them."

The next few afternoons followed a familiar pattern. Once Patrick made it home from school, Luke and Jefferson would usually talk him into rowing across the river with them to practice with the aborigine team at Dingo Creek. The two guests would usually have finished helping Mrs. McWaid for the day—catching up with firewood, repairing the leaking roof on the cabin, or cleaning up around the place.

On the Tuesday before the match, Patrick and Michael rode home from school with their neighbor Mr. Duggan. Becky had passed up the ride to work on an after-school project; she hadn't told him what.

"Heard an aborigine team is going to play our town boys this Saturday," Mr. Duggan said when Patrick had climbed into the wagon. "Sounds pretty funny, eh?"

Without thinking, Patrick smiled and chuckled along with the man.

Why did I do that? Patrick asked himself. *What am I afraid of?*

"Now, I don't have any problems with the aborigines," the man continued, as if he were telling a joke. "Fact, I've known some fine ones. But everyone knows they're not up to playing a complicated game like cricket, am I right?"

"I don't know." Patrick took a deep breath. "I . . . uh . . ." He wanted to kick himself for not defending the aborigines, but his tongue felt tied in knots.

"So are you going to the match?" asked Mr. Duggan as they neared the edge of town.

"Uh, the cricket match?" Patrick stalled. "No. I don't think so."

Mr. Duggan nodded, leaving Patrick to kick himself again. Becky ran up to the wagon then, waving for them to stop.

"Patrick!" she cried. "Wait!"

Startled, Mr. Duggan brought his two horses to a stop.

"What are you doing here, Becky?" asked Patrick.

Becky took a couple of moments to catch her breath, and she held on to her brother's ankle.

"You've got to come with me, Patrick," she puffed. "I need to show you."

"What are you talking about?"

Becky shook her head and looked at Mr. Duggan. "I'll explain it to you later."

Mr. Duggan smiled and nodded. "You go ahead, lad. I'll tell your mother you two will be walking home today."

Becky didn't wait for Patrick's answer, nearly pulling him off the wagon.

"What's this all about, Becky?" he asked, and when he saw Jefferson waiting for them around the corner in an alley, he dug in his heels. Jefferson waved him on, as if he were in as much of a hurry as Becky seemed to be.

"Look, the more people who see this, the easier it will be to convince the constable."

"Convince him of what?" Patrick wanted to know. "Becky, have you been playing police inspector again?"

Neither she nor Jefferson answered as they ran into the alley.

"And what are you doing here, Jeff?" Patrick tried another question. "I thought you were working on the cabin roof with Luke."

"We were," answered Jefferson. "But I had to come in for some supplies at Mullarky's, only the store didn't have the nails we needed. Then I ran into your sister."

"Quite a coincidence." Patrick knew it wasn't. And he frowned when he thought of Jefferson going out of his way to see Becky. But she returned Jefferson's smile as they followed her back to the center of town, up High Street, and around the block at Pakenham Street.

"Where are you leading us?" Patrick asked.

Becky kept looking up and down the streets, searching the late afternoon crowds. "Just tell me if you see anyone following us," she finally answered.

Patrick's eyes narrowed. "Becky, I don't think this is a good idea."

But Becky held up her hand and kept walking. Finally they

slipped down an alley, not far from the railroad tracks, and she walked even more quickly.

"Slow down, Becky," complained Patrick, feeling a pain in his side. "What is this?"

Halfway down the alley, Becky suddenly stopped and put her ear to the weathered boards of a stable. She looked quickly up and down the alley.

"Say, Becky—" Even Jefferson was wondering now.

"Look," said Patrick, rattling the handle of a barn-style door. "It's locked, and people don't want us—"

"Shh," she warned them, then she leaned down and pushed on a wide board. It swung in from the bottom, as if it were on a hinge, and she slipped inside the stable. Patrick looked at Jefferson.

"Do you know what she's doing?" asked Patrick.

Jefferson shook his head. "I know as much as you do, friend."

Becky motioned them inside. "Are you two boys going to stand out there all afternoon?"

With a shrug Jefferson slipped inside, and Patrick sighed as he followed them.

It took a moment for his eyes to adjust to the darkness. When they did, Patrick found they were standing in a rather sorry little stable, big enough only for three or four horses. By the shafts of light filtering in through cracks in the weathered siding, Patrick could make out a pile of bridles stacked carelessly in the corner. Jefferson whistled.

"Look over here," Becky told them, pointing toward the bridles. "Who do you think these belong to?"

"How should we know that?" Patrick put his hands on his hips. "Becky, is this what was so important that you had to drag me—"

"Don't you see?" Becky showed them one of the bridles. "These are stolen. They all belong to different owners. You can tell—look."

Jefferson bent closer for a better look, but Patrick only paced nervously.

"Why did you bring us here?" asked Patrick. "This isn't like you at all, Becky."

"I brought you here so you could help me convince the constable and pa and whoever else we have to convince."

"But convince them of what?"

Jefferson picked up a small metal can with a loose top that had been perched on a crude wooden shelf. "Hmm, what's this?" he mumbled.

"Probably for the horses," replied Patrick, not really paying attention. He peeked out through the boards. "Look, someone is going to see us in here. . . ."

"Don't worry so much." Jefferson dipped his finger into a black paste and made a face.

"That stuff smells like rotten eggs." Patrick tried to take the can from his friend but only got some of the gooey black stuff on his own hands. "Put it down, Jeff."

Jefferson returned to inspecting the bridles with Becky.

"I still don't understand." Patrick shook his head. "You sneak into a stable, and there are a lot of bridles. What did you expect?"

"But not this *many* bridles," Becky corrected him. "And not this."

Both boys stared at her when she lifted up a long stick in the half darkness.

"Let me see that," whispered Jefferson, taking what looked like an aborigine spear from her. Sure enough, when Patrick looked more closely, he could make out the sharp metal tip. There was no doubt who had made it.

"All right then," Patrick sighed. "It's an aborigine spear. That still doesn't prove anything. At least not anything I want to know about."

"Question is," said Jefferson, "does it still belong to an aborigine?"

"That's what I've been trying to explain to you," said Becky. "The other day when I was following—"

Patrick clamped his hand over his sister's mouth just then and pulled her back from the wall.

"Shh!" he warned her. "I think someone's coming!"

Outside they heard footsteps, then a soft rattle of the old padlock at the door. Jefferson pulled them slowly back, farther into the shadows.

Can we hide? wondered Patrick, frantically glancing around the stable. The boxes in the corner weren't big enough to hide behind, and there wasn't enough hay on the floor to cover anyone, even if it hadn't been dirty.

Becky motioned with her eyes for them to follow her to the back.

"This way," she whispered into his ear. "There's another way out the back."

They couldn't slip out quietly enough, though. A nail squeaked loudly as Becky held up a board in the wall. The man at the door behind them paused.

"Is anyone in here?" The voice sounded muffled, and Patrick couldn't recognize who it might be.

Jeff made it safely out, then Becky. Patrick ducked down to squeeze through the tiny opening and caught his shirt on a nail.

"Come on!" hissed Jefferson, yanking Patrick through. As his shirt ripped, Patrick glanced back to see a man's leg coming in through the other door.

"Hey, you!" yelled the man. "Stop right there!"

CHAPTER 11

WHO BELIEVES US?

"Split up!" Jefferson ordered. "Meet you at the *Herald*!"

Patrick went left, while Becky and Jefferson took the other way. They would have the shorter route to his father's newspaper office, but he was determined not to let them beat him.

Run! Patrick told himself as he sprinted away from the stable, down an alley, around a corner, and back toward town. Weaving in and out of horses and wagons on the street, he didn't slow down until he was standing in front of his father's newspaper office. Jefferson was already there, resting his hands on his knees to catch his breath, and Becky was just coming out with their father.

"Did you tell him?" panted Jefferson.

"Pa, a man was after us—" began Patrick, still out of breath.

"And we found all the bridles from the horses they've stolen," interrupted Becky. "I'm sure they're all stolen. They must be, but—"

"And then he nearly broke down the front doors—" added Jefferson. It had seemed that way to Patrick, too.

"And I saw his leg coming in through the door," Patrick put in at the same time.

Mr. McWaid held up his hands, trying to keep them from talking all at once.

"Wait, wait, wait," he told them, but the chatter only got louder until he put two fingers in his mouth and whistled loudly. They immediately stopped.

"That's better." Mr. McWaid straightened his vest. "Now, will just one of you mind telling me exactly what is going on? Becky, suppose you start first. And slowly, now, please."

Becky took a deep breath and straightened her skirt.

"All right."

"We should go inside, don't you think? I mean, just in case he followed us?" Patrick worried as he checked down the street. Nothing yet.

"He's not going to bother us here, whoever it was," Jefferson told them, and Becky began her story. She told Mr. McWaid about finding the old stable, about the spears and stolen things. Their father nodded the whole time and even took out his notebook from his back pocket as he listened.

"But then he discovered us," added Jefferson, and Becky allowed him to interrupt.

"There's more than likely a good explanation for this," said Mr. McWaid, but he wrote it all down in his reporter's notebook.

Jefferson nodded quickly. "Has to be, sir. We'll take you there if you want to see."

"Oh, I would, at that." Mr. McWaid looked carefully at his son and daughter, as if he were making sure they weren't hurt. "But we'll have one of the constables come with us."

He didn't even scold us for getting in trouble, Patrick thought as they hurried down the street to find Constable Fitzgerald. Fifteen minutes later they had managed to find the constable eating supper at the Wheatsheaf Hotel on Warren Street. Patrick was glad when their father quickly explained what they had found.

"I'll be there," he told them, wiping the gravy from the corner of his mouth with a white cloth napkin. "As soon as I finish this beefsteak."

When Becky didn't move from her spot next to his table, he sighed and pushed back his chair without looking up.

"Oh, very well, then, young lady. Let's see this den of thieves."

This time Patrick hung back, letting Becky and his father take

Constable Fitzgerald around the block and down the shadowy alley.

"I don't know why this couldn't wait," grumbled the constable. Their footsteps echoed off the brick walls on either side. And even though his father and the constable walked with them, Patrick felt his heart racing.

What if the thief is still around? he asked himself. He nearly yelped when he saw their own shadows move, then scolded himself for being so jumpy.

There's no one around anymore, he told himself.

"There it is," Becky pointed at the stable. "There's the hideout."

Constable Fitzgerald stopped and rubbed his eyes to get a better look. "Locked, I'm afraid."

"It's all there inside," insisted Becky. "Stolen things, I'm sure."

"Well . . ." The constable kicked at one of the boards with his foot. "I've probably walked by this old place dozens of times. Don't even know who it belongs to. But if this is some kind of joke . . ."

"My daughter would never play a joke like this." Mr. McWaid bent down to pick up one end of a board. "You can believe what she tells you."

Jefferson and Patrick pulled back the board that had served as a door. Constable Fitzgerald could hardly fit through the opening, but he stepped in after the boys.

"You kids had better be right about this," he mumbled, and they strained their eyes to see.

"Alex!" yelled a man from up in the alley. "Hold it there, Alex!"

It was Constable Mitchell, the constable's strong-armed young assistant. Patrick sighed with relief to see he was holding a lantern in his hand. When the younger man with the ruddy cheeks stepped past their father, a golden glow from his lantern spread out into the stable.

"I say, almost had the three ruffians just a few minutes ago," puffed Mitchell. "Heard there's been aborigines sneaking around in this stable. But they jumped out at me like a banshee and ran away. Three of them, I think there were."

Patrick finally recognized the voice as that of the man who had surprised them. Constable Mitchell!

"That was us," whispered Jefferson.

"What?" sputtered Constable Mitchell.

"That was *us* in here," said Patrick. "We thought you were one of the thieves."

"Me?" The constable snorted, drawing himself up even taller than he already was. "Well, if you had stopped the way I had ordered, we wouldn't have had this trouble, now, would we? Why, I've a good mind to speak to your parents about this."

Mr. McWaid cleared his throat, and Constable Fitzgerald took a good look at everyone, his lantern raised. "Yes, well, let's have a look in there. What's the meaning of all this?"

"We were trying to explain," replied Jefferson, pulling himself back against the wall of the stable so Constable Mitchell could squeeze in with his lantern. "This is where all the . . ."

His voice trailed off as the chief constable swung his lantern around. There was hay on the floor just like before, but . . .

"What happened to all the bridles?" asked Becky. "They were here just a few minutes ago."

"Perhaps in the dark, miss, your imagination could've got the better of you?" asked Constable Mitchell.

"That's not it at all!" said Jefferson. "There was an aborigine spear, too. I dropped it right . . ." He bent down to pick up a long stick, but it was only a long stick, perhaps a willow branch, cut from a tree along the river. "Right here."

"I used to pretend with such branches when I was young, too," snorted the young constable. "But I never confused the pretend with the real thing."

"We're not confused." Becky stood up straight. "We saw everything in here, just the way we told Constable Fitzgerald!"

"Look, miss." Constable Mitchell turned with his lantern to go. "I think you'd better give your imagination a rest. How long ago was it that I chased you all out of here? Twenty minutes ago? You really think someone could have come in here and cleaned out everything in that short time?"

"That's what must have happened." Patrick was as sure as his sister sounded.

"Humph." Constable Mitchell stepped out behind his boss while Jefferson felt around on the floor one last time. "Now, I can't abide you trespassing in this place any longer," Constable Mitchell went on, his voice turning even more serious than before. "No matter that it looks deserted. You kids clear out of here—and *stay* out."

Patrick reluctantly followed his sister, Mr. McWaid, and Jefferson out of the stable. They stopped and stood in the constable's lamplight.

"What do we do, Pa?" wondered Patrick, but their father could say nothing.

"Mitchell is right," said Constable Fitzgerald. "This is no place for you." He reached over and kicked at a board with his black boot and slapped the dust off his hands. "Besides, there may be rats and who knows what else in there," concluded the constable.

"We'd better get home," their father finally said. "Your mother is probably sitting there with Luke and Michael and a cold supper, wondering what happened to us. I'm sorry to trouble you, Constable."

By that time Patrick had seen enough. *They'll never believe us, no matter what we say.* He crossed his arms and turned away just in time to see a man on a horse gallop past the opening to the alley.

"Constable Fitzgerald!" A couple of other men ran by, then returned. "Constable Fitzgerald!"

"Down this way." The constable hurried out to the street to see who was calling him, and the others followed.

"You'd better hurry," said one of the men. "There's been a breakout at the jail."

"What?" grumbled Constable Fitzgerald. "If it's not one thing, it's another."

They all raced for the street, then turned right toward the jail. It wasn't long before Patrick saw a street full of lanterns and people running the same direction they were.

"Heard what's happening at the jail, Constable?" asked one older man limping down the street as fast as he could beside them. "I hear there's a whole army of black fellows there, tearing the place down."

"Let's just find out what happened when we get there," snapped the constable. He left them behind and ran the last block, straight toward the gathering crowd.

The people in front of the jail—mostly men from the saloons— looked as if they had come out to witness a fight. They cheered as Constable Fitzgerald pushed through to the front.

"Here he is," said one man, and the crowd cheered once more.

"Someone grab him!" cried a man at the front of the crowd of about twenty men.

Patrick ran behind the constable.

"Patrick!" warned his father, but Patrick had already pushed past two men to see what was going on.

Oh no! thought Patrick when he saw the dark, slumped figure of a young man—an aborigine man. In the light from a couple of lanterns, he could see the man was holding a long-handled ax, and he was kneeling next to the jail's side wall, away from direct view of the street. He could have been hiding next to the jail all night. But he was sobbing bitterly and wildly swinging the ax. Every time he hit the building, the wood siding would splinter loudly, and the crowd would jump.

"Someone stop the crazy fool," a man shouted, but no one dared go near. The constable hovered just a few steps away, trying to talk to him.

"Put down the ax," ordered Constable Fitzgerald, and the aborigine man glared back at them. He held the ax up and waved it uncertainly.

Patrick gasped when the light from a lantern fell across his face. "It's Matthew!" he told his sister, who had stepped up next to him.

"One of your cricket players?" she asked.

Patrick nodded and did the only thing he could think of. He stepped forward and past the constable, who tried to grab Patrick's arm but missed.

"Wait, Patrick," said Jefferson.

"Don't be foolish, boy," said the constable. "He's crazy."

"He's not crazy," Patrick answered quietly. "But he doesn't speak much English."

Patrick stepped forward slowly, his hand out.

"Matthew, it's me, Patrick McWaid. Remember? I'm the fellow who comes to watch your practices. Cricket."

Matthew took another vicious swipe at the side of the jail, ignoring Patrick and the others. The aborigines inside called out, but of course Patrick couldn't understand the words.

"No!" Constable Fitzgerald took a quick step forward but changed his mind when the young aborigine held up the ax again.

"He's trying to bust out his horse-thieving friends!" shouted one in the crowd.

Patrick tried to shut his ears to the crowd and crept forward. He did look over his shoulder once, though, to see his father pushing past Becky. Constable Fitzgerald held Mr. McWaid back.

"Matthew, don't do this." Patrick turned to plead again with the aborigine. "You don't need to do this. You're only making it worse for yourself."

But he doesn't understand a word I'm saying. Patrick kept his hand out as he crept forward. *Where's Moses when you need him?*

"Patrick!" yelled his father, but Patrick tried to keep his eyes locked on Matthew's.

Patrick took another step. Matthew kept the ax ready on his shoulder, ready to swing. He murmured a few angry words in his language, words that sounded an awful lot like the curses he had thrown at Patrick before.

"I know your brothers are still in jail," whispered Patrick, and the crowd had hushed. "But look, if they stole people's horses, that's what they deserve. And if they didn't . . . well, not much chance of that, but they'll get a fair trial."

Patrick swallowed hard and took another half step.

Matthew swayed with the axe over his head and grunted.

"No, Matthew." Patrick shook his head. "Listen, you've got to put down that ax."

He didn't even know what he would say next, but he went on anyway. "I promise you, Matthew. We'll make it right."

Patrick couldn't remember what else he said, but Matthew seemed finally to understand. Breathing hard, the aborigine stared straight into Patrick's eyes, as if looking for a friend.

With his last step Patrick reached up and grasped the ax handle. For a long moment they stood nose to nose, the ax waving slightly just above Patrick's head.

CHAPTER 12

ACCUSED

Let go of the ax! thought Patrick as his legs turned to water. Much longer, and Patrick knew he would collapse. *Just let go, Matthew.*

At last Matthew eased his grip. A woman gasped in the crowd behind them before Matthew finally let go of the ax and turned away.

The next few minutes were a blur for Patrick. He remembered strong hands rushing up behind him and lifting him off his feet, and he remembered the crowd closing in around them. But what he remembered most was the picture of Matthew on his knees in the dirt next to the jail wall. A dozen lanterns lit up the scene by that time, and Patrick would always remember the look of pain on Matthew's face and the tears that left tracks down his dusty cheeks.

"I promise you, Matthew," Patrick repeated as his father and Jefferson led him away from the crowd of people. "I promise."

Patrick remembered one other thing from that evening: the sight of Sebastian Weatherby standing at the edge of the crowd, his arms crossed as the constable led Matthew into the jail with his friends. Sebastian's pleasure was obvious.

"Don't look at him," warned Becky, but Patrick didn't need any coaching to follow her advice this time.

Patrick tossed and turned that night. He dozed in snatches, only to be wakened by voices outside early the next morning, Wednesday. Only a few dull golden clouds over the tops of the river trees told Patrick it was morning.

"See here, Mr. McWaid, I know you're a respected member of the community." Patrick recognized Constable Fitzgerald's voice. The front door was slightly open, letting in the cool, damp morning air. It smelled like the river, and he shivered.

"Mr. Field at the newspaper thinks highly of you and your family," continued the constable, "and of course you've been cleared of the crime that brought you to Australia in the first place."

"Is that Constable Fitzgerald out there, John?" their mother asked as she stepped outside. Becky and Michael followed, while Patrick kept watch by the door. "You're just in time for a little breakfast, Constable."

"Thank you, no." The constable pulled nervously at his long mustache and made no move to get off his horse. "As I said, Mrs. McWaid, everyone thinks highly of your husband, but I'm only doing my job."

"Come on, Alexander." Mr. McWaid shielded his children with his arm. After the night before with the ax-swinging Matthew, Patrick knew his father wouldn't take any chances.

"All right, sir." The constable puffed up his chest a bit. "Let me spell it out for you. You know we've had some problems with horse thefts lately. Some we believe were stolen by aborigines."

"No, it's—" Becky began, but her father put up his hand.

"I'm sorry," Mr. McWaid apologized. "Go on."

"Yes, well, as I was saying, some of the aborigines are causing us headaches. But we have reason to believe that they are being used in a much larger scheme."

"What kind of scheme?" asked Mr. McWaid. Patrick held on to his father's arm.

The constable went on. "The people behind the theft ring use aborigines to steal the horses, so the aborigines are the ones who are seen. But the horses are taken to a collection point far out in the bush, then across state lines. Sometimes young people ride the horses across, so as not to arouse suspicion. It's been done in New South Wales. Very clever."

"That's all very well, Constable," replied their father. "But what has that to do with us?"

"That's just it." The constable shifted in his saddle. "We've received reports that your son was seen taking a stolen horse from a local farm."

Mr. McWaid groaned. "Oh, come now, Alexander. Can't you recognize more lies when you hear them? This is getting preposterous. Now they're stealing the animals and inducing children to ride them to collection points? It's, it's—"

"It's hard to believe, I know." The constable finished Mr. McWaid's sentence. "But you understand I have to do my job. I'd like your permission, if you please, to search your outbuilding."

Mr. McWaid shook his head and sighed. "If it will make you feel better. But this feels just like yesterday, doesn't it?"

"Yes, but we also had a few questions about your son's . . . er . . . the incident last night at the jail."

Patrick bit his lip. His father had already given him a long lecture about what he had done.

"My assistant, Mitchell, even questioned your children having us investigate an empty stable on one side of town at the same time that distressed fellow tried to chop his friends out of jail on the other side of town."

"Oh, come." Mr. McWaid clucked his tongue as they walked around the house. "You're not saying my children had anything to do with that? You and your assistant are talking as if the children are common criminals. This is growing more and more absurd all the time."

"Quite," answered the constable. "And yet it's known that your children have spent a good deal of time in the company of, well . . ."

Patrick knew what the man was going to say, and he was glad for once that Luke wasn't around to hear it. Maybe he was off for a morning walk. The constable and Mr. McWaid led them in silence to the little shed behind the cabin. The shed, which had no windows, was covered over in river bluebell vines and stood not much bigger than their outhouse.

"This is where Christopher sleeps when it's cold and rainy," explained Michael. His koala perched on his shoulder with a leaf in its mouth.

"Christopher?" The constable looked interested until their father explained that Christopher was the animal riding on his son's shoulder. The shed door screeched as Becky turned a rusty latch and pulled it open.

"See here?" explained Mr. McWaid. "My father just keeps a number of tools out here. . . ."

His voice trailed off as they all saw the morning sun fall on two full sets of horse bridles, a shiny silver bit, and reins. Patrick stared at them, and then he knew.

"Pa, those are the bridles we saw in the stable yesterday."

"I see," said the constable, pulling the reins down from a hook on the wall. "That's a nice touch, now. Have any horses here, do you?"

"You know we don't, Alexander." Mr. McWaid's face started to turn red. "I don't quite know what's going on here, but I'm telling you—"

"Pa—" interrupted Patrick.

Jefferson, Luke, and Mrs. McWaid appeared around the corner of the shed.

"What's the problem, John? The children need to go to school." Patrick's mother held three metal lunch buckets in her hand. Her clear green eyes flashed with concern as she looked at her husband.

"There's no problem, Sarah. But we seem to have a prankster." His eyes narrowed and he turned back to the constable. "You know, of course, we'd never do such a thing, don't you, Alexander?"

"I know that personally, Mr. McWaid. Of course I do." The constable scratched his head and held the bridles out in front of him as he spoke. "But word is that you're a little short of cash, and one could see how a man in that kind of situation might be tempted to—"

"How can anyone *say* such a thing? After all we've been through." Mrs. McWaid burst into tears and ran back to the cabin, dragging Becky along with her.

"Now . . . wait, Mrs. McWaid," the constable stuttered while Mr. McWaid glared at the man, his hands on his hips. Patrick was almost afraid to look. Michael was off chasing Christopher, who had begun to climb up a nearby gum tree.

"I'm required to make a report of this," Constable Fitzgerald finally whispered. He squeezed the leather bridle between his hands.

"Fine. You write that someone is trying to make it look as if the McWaid family is involved in horse theft. You write that the real— what do you call them here in Australia—the *real* gully-rakers are still out there raking gullies, or stealing horses. Put *that* in your report. Good day, Constable."

With that he took Patrick's arm and marched back to the cabin. The constable disappeared down the lane without another word. Jefferson and Luke were silent.

"Why are you so mad, Pa?" squeaked Michael.

"I don't fancy to being accused like that." Their father was still red in the face as he waved a long, bony finger in their faces. "But now, you two, I've had quite enough of this business. After last night, and now this escapade—"

"John, you can't blame them," put in Mrs. McWaid, drying her tears.

Patrick couldn't remember seeing his father this angry. Not for a long time.

"And why not?" their father shot back as he marched to the window and peeked through a crack in the the boards he had nailed there to keep the cold out. "Why can't I blame them?"

"Pa, I'm sorry," began Becky, and Mr. McWaid's shoulders sagged as he looked at his daughter.

"So am I, Rebecca. I just don't want you to get mixed up in something where you could get hurt. Do you understand what I'm saying?"

Becky nodded. Jefferson poked his nose in the door with Luke, then backed out quickly as Mr. McWaid turned to Patrick.

"And as for you, young man . . ."

Patrick winced, waiting for the words to hit him.

"Let me count what's happened since you sneaked away to the corroboree that night." As his father paced the floor, he started counting on his fingers. "We've had a visit from a little aborigine boy—who knows *what* happened to him. We've had our windows broken out by troublemakers unknown. Your mother's upset. And now the police suspect *us* of horse thievery!"

"Yes, sir," Patrick managed to squeak. "That's why we need to go back to Dublin."

Their father groaned. "Not *that* again, Patrick. Come, now—we can solve this . . . together."

The front door burst open, and Michael appeared out of breath.

"Pa, could you help me get Christopher out of a tree? He's stuck."

"Not now, Michael!" snapped Mr. McWaid.

"Sorry." Michael backed away. "I'll try myself."

"Your father didn't mean anything, dear," said Mrs. McWaid, holding out one of the lunch pails to Michael. "He's just a bit upset. Now, take your lunch and wait for Patrick and Becky. They'll be out in just a minute. I'll check on the animal."

By this time Patrick was afraid to move, afraid to say anything else besides "yes, sir."

"Have you anything to say for yourself?" his father finally asked after Michael had taken his lunch and escaped back outside.

"Remember the last verse we read together, Pa?" Becky asked quietly.

Patrick couldn't get any words past his throat. He knew he would break out in tears if he did, and he couldn't remember how long it had been since he had done that.

Not in front of Pa, he promised himself. *Not now*.

His father stopped to look at Becky and frowned.

"What verse do you mean, dear?" His voice suddenly softer. Mrs. McWaid looked away and shaded her eyes, the way she always did when she was about to cry.

"You didn't forget, did you, Pa?" Becky stepped over to the table next to their mother and father's bed, where the family Bible was kept. The Bible their mother had brought all the way over from Ireland with her.

"We were just trying to obey that verse." Becky leafed quickly through the book, her hands trembling, until she found the spot she was looking for, near the back of the Bible. No one said a word as she turned it around and pointed it out to her father. "Here."

Of course Patrick knew which verse his sister was talking about, even if his father seemed to have forgotten. It hadn't been so long ago that they had read it together.

" 'Therefore to him that knoweth to do good, and doeth it not . . .' " Their father read quietly, then looked up from the page with moist eyes. He finished the verse without looking down. " '. . . to him it is sin.' "

A bird screeched outside.

"I remember." Their father took a deep breath, and the color drained from his cheeks.

"We'll be fine, Pa." Becky gave her father a hug, but Patrick couldn't bring himself to approach his father. He could still feel the wall between them.

"Patrick!" shouted Michael, just outside the door. "Becky! We're going to be late for school."

"Go then." Mrs. McWaid held out their pails for them. Probably a hard-boiled egg and his mother's delicious thick-sliced bread.

"Thanks, Ma." Patrick looked back at his father.

"We'll talk about this again later," Mr. McWaid told them.

Patrick, Michael, and Becky walked through the eucalyptus trees that surrounded their cabin without saying anything. Michael skipped ahead, exploring rotting logs or animal holes until they caught up, and then he would skip ahead again. Finally they neared the town.

"Does this mean you're not going to help the aborigines play cricket anymore?" Michael asked at last.

"Michael!" Becky frowned. "Were you listening to what Pa was saying?"

"How could I not?" answered Michael. "He was yelling so loudly."

"Hmm." Patrick didn't answer Michael's question but picked his way carefully between mud puddles on the street leading to their school. Becky did the same, choosing her own path but keeping up with him. He was glad she didn't say much; he wouldn't have had much to tell her. His mind felt about as clear as the mud under his feet, so he just gritted his teeth and steered clear of the worst. Sometimes he would back up to get a running start to vault over a wider puddle, as Becky took the long way around.

Even when they were still on the outskirts of town, they could tell that Echuca was coming alive for the day. When he listened, Patrick could hear the shouts of men driving their wagons, the clatter and splash of hooves in the streets. "Coming through!" yelled a wagon driver. A horse whinnied. And someone was hammering nails.

Is a new building going up? Patrick wondered. Anything to get his mind off what had happened to them that morning,

Then, without warning, something whistled past Patrick's ear, barely missing.

"Oh!" Becky shrieked next to him on the side of the road.

When he looked over, he saw his sister sway dangerously as she grabbed the side of her head.

CHAPTER 13

THE NATURAL

"Becky!" Patrick cried, reaching over to keep his sister from falling. Something else whistled by, missing Patrick's head by mere inches. A rotten apple hit the dirt street beside them and rolled off into the roadside ditch.

"You can't do that!" hollered Michael into a nearby alley. Patrick thought he heard laughing in the distance. Michael picked up a rock, as if to throw it at the attackers.

"Don't, Michael," said Patrick, helping Becky wipe the rotten apple off her cheek. Her entire face was red, and she bent over as if she was going to be sick.

"Are you all right?" he asked.

"I'm all right," she told him.

"They can't do that," insisted Michael, hopping up and down.

"Did you see who threw it?" Patrick asked.

No one else on the street seemed to notice them as a delivery wagon with four hefty draft horses lumbered past. The driver wrestled the reins and looked straight ahead. The hammering continued as a new storefront went up just ahead.

"I didn't see them," replied Michael. "But I saw where the apples came from. One almost hit me, too."

Patrick nodded as his sister smoothed her dress down and looked around. "It was Sebastian and his friends. Had to be."

"Why would they do that?" Michael wondered out loud. "What did we ever do to them?"

"I surely don't know, Michael." When Becky set her jaw and marched ahead, they had to run to keep up. "But now it's what we're still going to do that's going to make them upset."

After school Patrick and Becky mapped out their next steps as they hurried through the streets toward home. This time Michael looked both ways each time they came to a street or an alley, anywhere fruit-throwing enemies could be hiding in ambush.

"They're not going to get us this time," he told them, crossing his arms. "I'll be the scout."

"I feel better with you on guard, little brother." Becky smiled, and Patrick could see she still had a red mark on the cheek where the apple had hit her.

She looked at Patrick. "So you're going back to Dingo Creek?"

Patrick shrugged his shoulders. "I don't know. What about you? What are you going to do?"

"I still have to find out who was *really* stealing horses, especially now they think it might be *you*, Patrick."

"Come, now." Patrick shook his head. "This whole affair is too crazy to believe."

"Didn't you hear the constable? He was serious. Someone *did* say they saw you with a stolen horse. There's more to this than you think. Much more."

Patrick wondered what else his sister knew, but he didn't dare ask her any more questions as they walked home. Instead, he hurried to meet Jefferson and Luke at Dingo Creek.

"Can I go with you this time?" Michael asked when Patrick tossed his red-covered schoolbook on the front porch. Patrick looked around quickly.

"No, Michael. The other boys are waiting for me."

Patrick ran for the river, at first hoping his brother wouldn't follow, then stopped.

"If you're coming, you have to keep up."

Michael smiled at him as they raced down to the riverbank where the rowboat was usually tied.

"There you are," said Luke, leaning against a tree.

With a quick shove Patrick pushed the boat into the water and rowed as hard as he could. Jefferson and Luke chatted as they walked to Dingo Creek, but Patrick was two steps ahead of them the whole time.

"What's your hurry?" asked Jefferson.

"I have a bad feeling about this," Patrick answered quietly. When they walked out to the clearing, he saw what he thought they would see. An empty field.

"Where is everyone?" asked Michael, looking puzzled. "Isn't this where you practice?"

"Used to be," replied Patrick, and he walked up to where the wickets were usually set up.

"Hullo!" shouted Michael. "We're here!"

"Michael—" Patrick tried to quiet his brother, then shrugged. "Oh well, what does it matter anyway? Matthew is in jail now. And without him . . ."

"We don't have much of a chance," finished Luke, putting into words what no one had yet dared to say.

But it was true, and they all knew it.

"He was our best batsman." Luke reached down, picked up the ball, and tossed it up and down. "Best bowler, too. Why did he do something so . . . so stupid?"

"I wish I could tell you," answered Moses, and Patrick jumped. He hadn't heard the blind man approaching. "But some of our people believe it was you who brought all the trouble on us."

"You think that's true?" Patrick couldn't believe what he was hearing.

"No." Moses shook his head sadly. "No, I don't. But the people . . ."

"Me?" Patrick still shook his head. "All I've been doing is watching."

Without warning Luke threw the ball at Patrick—not underarm-style as he had already taught them, but almost sidearm and with his elbow locked—as if he were throwing a spear. Patrick took a vicious swipe at the ball with the bat he was holding.

Luke ducked and covered his head, but he needn't have worried. The ball sailed over Luke, over Jefferson and Michael, even over Moses at the edge of the field.

"What kind of a bowl was that?" asked Patrick. "You looked as if you were throwing a javelin!"

"Never mind that," Luke told him as Michael trotted into the bushes to find the ball. "Let me see you hit that again."

"A new kind of bowling and a home run," whistled Jefferson, looking in amazement from where Patrick stood to where the ball had sailed out of sight. Michael was still searching the bushes. "I've never seen anyone hit it *that* far before."

"That was a six, it was." Luke shook his head while Patrick looked down at the bat to double-check if it was really his hands that were holding the bat.

"It was just an accident," he told them.

Michael whooped when he finally came back with the ball. "You really sent that one, Patrick," his little brother told him. "Do it again."

Patrick shook his head. "I can't. I told you it was just an accident."

But Luke didn't listen. He just wound up and pitched the ball again the same way.

Patrick saw the ball coming fast, straight for his knee. In one swift move he stepped backward and swatted upward in an arc. Once more, the ball sailed high over Moses.

"I heard that one!" commented the silver-haired man with a smile.

Michael hollered once again as he raced after the ball.

"Just an accident, eh?" Luke looked at him and smiled, and Michael rolled the ball back to him. "I think it's more than an accident."

Patrick knocked one pitch after the other far and high—three, six, ten times. Each time, Michael would faithfully trot out and retrieve the ball. And each time, a few more aborigine boys from the team would show up to watch.

"Look, they're all coming back!" shouted Jefferson, dragging one more player by the arm. As soon as they saw Patrick hitting the ball, they all started to smile and point, then cheer. A few of them picked up fist-sized stones and started to imitate Luke's new bowling style.

"Just a few more!" said Jefferson once the rest of the team had gathered around.

Patrick managed a small grin and sent another pitch blazing over Luke's head.

"How do you do that?" asked Luke. Patrick shrugged. "I thought you said you had never touched a cricket bat."

"I haven't." Patrick shook his head. "Quite odd, actually."

One of the aborigine players shouted, and they all cheered.

"What did he say?" Patrick asked Moses, who was grinning at the batting show.

"They all agree you should replace Matthew."

Patrick dropped the bat and took a step backward. "No! Is that what you're thinking? I can't do that."

"Why not?" asked Luke.

"I just couldn't." Patrick turned to go. "And I don't think it would be legal, being an all-aborigine team and all."

"Just as legal as bowling overhand," Luke told him.

"Legal?" repeated Moses. "Where is it written?"

"That's just it," said Luke. "We can do it."

A shout from the bush made all the aborigines turn around, and a small white man stepped into the clearing. He was wearing a blue blazer and a cream-colored hat cocked back off his sweaty brow, and he smiled when he saw Patrick.

"You Patrick McWaid?"

The man must have followed them to Dingo Creek. Patrick stared back at him and waited for him to wade through the crowd of curious aborigine children.

"The name's Foster." He mopped his brow with a handkerchief, even though it wasn't hot. "August Foster, with the *Melbourne*

Sunday Times. I was in town for a story on the railroad and heard about this cricket match on Saturday. I've come to do a story on you and your team."

Patrick shook the man's clammy hand and looked him over.

"I don't mind telling you I had a terrible time finding you," admitted Mr. Foster. "Almost ready to give up when I heard a lot of loud voices out here in the bush. This is a wild place for a cricket match, it is."

"Dingo Creek," said Luke.

The reporter jotted it down in his notebook. "Perfect," replied Foster, his face lighting up. "We'll call your team the Dingo Creek Eleven."

"Patrick was just helping us get ready for the match on Saturday." said Moses, who came up to meet the newspaperman.

"We are?" asked Patrick, looking at the Dingo Creek Eleven, minus Matthew. He couldn't tell by the way they stared back at him if Moses was just being hopeful or if there was a secret they weren't telling.

"He speaks English?" Foster turned to Patrick as Moses began discussing something in aborigine with the other ten fellows on the cricket team. They continued back and forth for the next several minutes. "What are they saying?"

Patrick could only shrug in response.

A couple of the players asked Moses questions, which he seemed to answer patiently enough. Finally they all looked at one another, as if they were voting. One by one they ran out onto the field, found their positions, and started throwing the ball around.

"They're not terribly interested in your newspaper, Mr. Foster," Moses finally said, looking halfway up at the sky the way he often did. "But I can probably answer most of your questions. As I said, they seem to be taken up with the idea of preparing for a match."

"Splendid!" Foster grinned and removed a large notebook from his back pocket, the same way Patrick had seen his father do so many times. He licked his pencil and began asking Moses questions like "How long have you been practicing the game?" and "Have any of you ever seen an actual cricket match?"

To the second question Moses answered that he had seen an actual match in his head, described to him by his grandson, his eyes.

"What will they do if they lose?" asked Foster, and Patrick was relieved he hadn't said "*when* they lose."

Moses scratched his chin thoughtfully. "I can't answer that question. But I understand the boys are good players."

Foster scribbled wildly on his notebook, recording every word. Next the newspaper reporter turned to him.

"You're the coach?" he asked Patrick.

Patrick pointed to Jefferson, who was standing next to one of the younger players, guiding him through a swing. Luke was throwing the ball while two of the players took turns hitting. Several more were gathered around them, offering their own advice and cheers.

"Luke's over there," said Patrick, pointing at his friend. "He's from another tribe. He's the coach, along with Jefferson, the other white fellow over there. I just get in the way."

Moses laughed. "Don't believe a word he's saying. We're still trying to convince him to play."

I don't think so, thought Patrick.

By the time Foster left an hour later, Patrick had returned to the practice with the others, and Jefferson had taught them all to shout "Home run!" every time they heard the crack of a bat and saw the ball sailing out of the oval playing field. They had even started laughing again, the way they always had before.

"It's not a home run!" insisted Luke. "Jefferson, you're confusing the matter."

"I don't think they're a bit confused, are you, boys?" Jefferson grinned, but his grin faded when he saw another group of visitors.

"Who invited them?" he muttered, and Patrick turned to see Sebastian Weatherby with Will and two of the other players from the town team. They just stood at a distance, saying nothing but watching everything.

"Just ignore them!" yelled Patrick. "Moses, tell them to just ignore them."

"Ignore who?" Moses asked back.

But over the next half hour, they could not ignore the four un-invited guests. Sebastian would chuckle at a missed ball or a wide throw, and his three followers would join in.

"They're just trying to make you fear them, can't you see?" Patrick picked up the cricket ball and tossed it back to a batsman who was having trouble. Of course, the boy didn't understand. He just kept looking over at Sebastian, who was mocking them with his crooked smile. Finally Sebastian laughed again before turning on his heel and leaving.

"It's getting dark," shouted Jefferson.

"Good practice." Luke looked over at Moses, who seemed to be snoozing in a hollowed-out stump of an ancient gum tree. It reminded Patrick of a throne. "We'll see you tomorrow."

They did see them the next day, Thursday, but it turned out to be a repeat of Wednesday. Sebastian and his friends showed up, laughed at every mistake, and left without a word. By that time Patrick knew he couldn't take any more.

"Good catch!" commented Luke when one of the aborigine players made a spectacular diving stop. Patrick had to admit that all of the boys on the team seemed to be able to run a little faster and jump a little higher than anyone he had ever seen. But the big match was the day after next. It would take more than a few good catches to win.

"Do you think the team actually has a chance Saturday?" Patrick asked Luke and Jefferson when they were walking home.

"If we don't," answered Jefferson, blowing out a deep breath, "we've sure taught a lot of aborigines a pretty useless game."

"Well, they'll be famous, anyway," Patrick told them. "That newspaper reporter from Melbourne is covering the match as if it were a world-class matchup."

"Just wait." Luke quickened his step. "We'll show everyone."

Patrick wondered just how they would do that as they crossed the river toward home.

"There's your sister." Jefferson pointed beyond the cabin at Becky, who was running up the lane in a flash of flying skirt and wavy nut-brown hair. She didn't notice when a paper that she carried fluttered out behind her and dropped to the ground.

"Becky!" cried Jefferson, scrambling up the bank. "You dropped something!"

But Becky didn't hear and didn't wait up, so Jefferson hurried to scoop up her paper and follow her inside. They found Mr. McWaid sitting at the table with his glasses on, writing with a simple ink pen.

"This is what I've been working on the past few days, Pa." Becky was out of breath. "Could you please read it?"

Becky shoved a piece of paper in front of her father on the table; Jefferson added the one that had fallen to the ground.

"You dropped this one," he told her, and she smiled back at him shyly.

On purpose, thought Patrick, but he didn't say anything. He just looked over his sister's shoulder to see the papers, but she shrugged to keep him from getting a better view. The story, or whatever it was, had been written and rewritten several times on the back side of an old advertisement for Holloway's Pills, "The Great Household Medicine That Ranks Among the Leading Necessities of Life, Purifying the Blood and Giving Tone, Energy, and Vigor." On Becky's side of the paper, tiny words were written sideways and in between the lines with Becky's fine, careful handwriting.

Their father set his work aside and slowly picked up Becky's paper with a careful half smile.

"An assignment for school?" he asked. "A story?"

Becky shook her head no. "It's what I've learned about the gully-rakers," she told them. "About the hideout, where we saw the spear. And about Ruth Wilson and what she told us."

Her voice got softer as they watched Mr. McWaid read. He held it sideways and picked out the sentences with his finger, nodded, and saying "m-hmmm" and "yes" as he read.

Becky looked at her brother with her eyebrows up, which meant a question was coming. Finally Mr. McWaid put the story back down.

"So you like it?" she asked. "Do you think it's . . . well . . . good enough to put in the newspaper?"

Mr. McWaid smiled. "I should have known that's what you were doing, Becky."

"Is that why it says 'By Becky McWaid' at the top?" By that time Michael was listening in.

"Well?" Even Patrick was waiting for the verdict.

"Your article is very well written, Becky." Their father carefully measured out his words. "You have a very nice and clear way of expressing yourself. Yes, very fine, indeed."

"So you like it?" Becky still didn't look sure of her father's approval. He held up his hand.

"I'm afraid it needs . . . well . . . it lacks substantiation, dear."

"Sub-what?" asked Michael.

"Substantiation." Patrick's father handed Becky her paper. "If you report a fact, you can't just let it go at that. You must quote a reliable person who can prove it."

"But, Pa," Becky objected, "anyone with sense can see—"

"Aye, anyone with sense, but that's not what writing in a newspaper is all about. You need proof. You need evidence. You need more people who will back up what you're writing, or else it just seems like your opinion."

Becky looked near tears. She crumpled up her paper and threw it on the floor.

"Don't do that, Becky!" Jefferson told her as he stooped down to retrieve her story. "It's good."

"Of course it is." Mr. McWaid took Becky's hand. "Listen, here's what we'll do. You talked to Ruth Wilson once."

Becky nodded her head.

"Well, go out there again and ask her a few more questions. Tell her you're working for the *Riverine Herald*, and see what she says."

Becky looked up with a puzzled expression. "Why would you want me to do that?"

"Let's just say I've hired you as my personal assistant." Their father grinned. "So if you can prove what you're trying to say here, I'll talk to Mr. Field at the paper and see if we can't run your article, or at least an article like it."

"Pa! Do you mean it?" Becky's expression had turned from night to day.

"I do, but you have to promise me you'll stay out of trouble. Now, here, I'll show you a thing or two about interviewing people."

Patrick groaned quietly. *Here she goes again*. He listened quietly from his cot while Becky and his father talked about how to ask questions, how to write it all down, how to find out what a person was really thinking. Once in a while, Becky would peek around the curtains at him to make sure he was listening. He was. But by the time they all stopped talking and his father had blown out their little oil lamp later that night, Patrick could have kicked himself for what he had agreed to do the next day.

CHAPTER 14

WASTED INVESTIGATION

Friday afternoon arrived too quickly for Patrick, but he had promised his sister to help her, and help her he would. Why he had promised he couldn't say.

Maybe I was talking in my sleep, he told himself, but it didn't matter.

"All right," he sighed as they walked down the street. "Let's get this over with. I said I'd help you."

The little cabin where Ruth Wilson lived looked even more overgrown and neglected than the first time Patrick and Becky had been there. And just like before, Mrs. Wilson's huge dog came charging out at them, stopped only by the leaning fence.

"Look, Becky," said Patrick stiffly. "I still don't see what you're going to find out by coming here one more time. You're just going to get in trouble."

"That's why you said you'd come, remember?" She grinned as if she had just told a joke. "You were going to protect me."

Patrick remembered, and he looked around for the tenth time to make sure no one had seen them coming. Finally he took a deep breath, pulled the gate back, and stared straight at the dog. Patrick smiled and held out his arms, just as Luke had once told him to do.

"Don't make him angry," his sister warned him, but the dog

only inched backward as they slowly made their way across the small pasture and then up to the house to stand in front of the door. In time, the beast disappeared around the back.

"Mrs. Wilson?" called Becky. "May we speak with you again?"

"Go away!" shouted the old woman from behind her door. "I've already told you everything I know."

"But, Mrs. Wilson." Becky wasn't about to give up. "I'm working for the *Riverine Herald* now. And I just have a couple of questions for you."

This time the woman cracked open the door and peeked out of her crooked shack while her dog growled from behind her. He must have retreated into the house through a back door. For a moment the old woman seemed to consider what Becky had told her, then she stepped back and fell over her dog with a cry.

"Mrs. Wilson!" Patrick was closest; he jumped to grab the woman's outstretched hand before she tumbled over backward. Before he knew what had happened, he was staring straight into Mrs. Wilson's startled eyes.

"Thank you, young man." Mrs. Wilson blurted out the words before she could catch herself. Patrick let go of her hand and looked down, almost embarrassed, as she sent the dog whimpering to a corner with a few sharp words.

"That animal is always in the way. Of course, my eyesight isn't all that it once was, either. I always seem to be tripping over bones or stones he brings in and leaves on the floor. I don't even know why I keep him around, except that he always lets me know when someone is at the door. Barks and barks at any little noise. Never fails. Now, you're Will's friends, aren't you?"

Patrick cleared his throat and peeked over to see what his sister would do. Mrs. Wilson had clearly forgotten who they were.

"Not exactly, ma'am," said Becky. "I'm doing a story for the *Herald*, and I need to know again about your missing horses."

Remember what Pa told you, Becky. Give her a chance to tell you her side of the story.

But Mrs. Wilson straightened her back almost the way a dog's hair stiffens at danger.

"If that's who you are, you should have said so in the first place." The woman practically spit the words their direction.

"I did, ma'am, but you must not have heard. I'm sorry." Becky took out her piece of paper and her pencil stub.

"People are saying that one of the aborigines who took your horses might still be on the loose," continued Becky, sounding more and more like a newspaper reporter. "Do you know anything about that?"

"Will says—" the woman caught herself. "I mean, no. All I know is that I saw the two."

"Did you know the men in jail have families who are worried about them?" asked Becky, standing up. Patrick wondered what his sister was getting at as she walked to the door.

"Can't be helped." Mrs. Wilson straightened her skirt. "They should have thought of that before they resorted to thievery."

"We want you to meet a friend, Mrs. Wilson." Becky motioned out the door.

What is she doing? wondered Patrick.

A moment later an aborigine boy appeared at the door, his hands behind his back—Davey! At first he wouldn't come in, but Becky coaxed him forward with a kind word. Patrick noticed Luke and Jefferson in the background, and Jefferson winked at him before they backed away.

"Who is this urchin?" Mrs. Wilson sputtered.

"His name is Davey," said Becky, warming up like a lawyer about to defend her client. "See his bandaged head? Your nephew and his friends did that. My father had to stitch his cut back together."

"Oh, Will would never do such a thing. He's a good boy, he is. Brings me a ham now and again." Mrs. Wilson rose to her feet. "And he's my only flesh and blood since his mother passed away. I've raised him as my own."

"Mrs. Wilson, can't you tell us what really happened that night your horses were stolen? It's not possible to see across your yard in the dark. There wasn't even a moon that night, it was so cloudy.

And you said your dog wasn't barking. Doesn't that give you a clue?"

But Mrs. Wilson wasn't listening; she seemed to be far away. "Even if Will did do what you said, I'm sure it was an accident."

"Please, Mrs. Wilson," answered Becky. "I don't know exactly what happened. But I don't think it was an accident. And you must tell us the truth. Can't you—"

"No!" thundered Mrs. Wilson, suddenly shaking like an autumn leaf. She wouldn't look at Davey as he stood in the doorway, confused. "I've seen enough."

Becky didn't answer for a moment, letting her words sink in. Patrick still said nothing, only prayed that Mrs. Wilson wouldn't have a heart attack on the spot as her jaw worked up and down.

"But, Mrs. Wilson," began Becky again.

"That's quite enough, young lady. You have a lot of nerve to come bursting into my home like this. Now, you take your brother and your young friend and clear out of here this instant!"

Davey looked wide eyed from Becky to Mrs. Wilson, and for a moment Patrick wanted to tell him all was well, but of course it wasn't.

"Please think about it, Mrs. Wilson," Becky pleaded while Davey slipped out the door.

"Naught to think about." Mrs. Wilson pushed Patrick from behind. "Now, get out. I don't want to see you around my property again!"

"I'm truly sorry, Mrs. Wilson," said Becky, her voice softening as the door to the shack slammed in their faces. They could hear the dog growling again on the other side. "We just wanted to find out the truth. We just wanted to help you."

"Help me and help yourself by leaving and never coming back," whimpered Mrs. Wilson from behind the door. Suddenly, she sounded much older and less angry than before. "If Will ever finds out I was talking to you . . . Will, he's all I have. . . ."

Mrs. Wilson broke into sobs, and there was nothing to do but leave the frightened old lady alone. They turned away from the house and hurried down the road. Not a minute later Patrick heard footsteps running up behind him.

"Wait for us!" called Jefferson.

Patrick looked around quickly to see Jefferson and Luke running to catch up with them. They held Davey's hands between them, carrying him like a toy. It had begun to rain.

"Well?" asked Jefferson as they caught up. "How did we do?"

"That was a disaster," admitted Becky as they trudged home. "A complete and total disaster."

"That good?"

"I don't think I'm going to be writing any newspaper stories," replied Becky. "Not after this."

As they walked, Patrick looked up at the gray clouds and tried to follow the big rain drops as they fell toward his face. After a time, talk turned to the cricket match.

"You *do* think we're going to win, don't you, Patrick?" asked Becky.

Patrick frowned. "I have a bad feeling about it."

"Why?" asked Jefferson, a slight smile playing at his lips. "You're not saying the Dingo Creek Eleven are going to lose, are you?"

"This whole thing is ridiculous," Patrick blurted out. He felt himself about to say something he would probably later regret. "The game is stupid. The entire idea is stupid. And this whole stupid affair would not have happened if we were back home in Dublin where we belong!"

Patrick started to run, but Jefferson's words stopped him cold.

"That's right, Patrick. Run away. Isn't that what you always do?"

A little shocked, Patrick froze, not turning around. "What do you know about it?"

"Enough to know that it's your standard reaction. It's what you always do about now."

"Yes?" Patrick finally twirled around to face the others. "Well, in Dublin—"

"That's part of your problem, too. You're stuck on this idea that everything would be perfect if only you were back in Dublin. Well, you're *not* back home in Dublin, or did you forget that, Patrick McWaid?"

"I've forgotten nothing." Patrick stamped his foot.

"So what's wrong with you, then?" Jefferson wasn't letting up. "Here your sister is trying to help out, and you're standing in her way. At least she's trying to *do* something."

"Jeff," whispered Becky. "That's enough."

"No, it's *not* enough." Jefferson's face was red. "I want to know what's wrong with you, because you're not the same Patrick McWaid I used to know."

"You don't understand."

"No? Well, I think I *do* understand. You're yellow. That's all. You're too afraid to stand up for anything."

Jefferson's words stung.

"And another thing. You always used to tell me about the 'Christian' thing to do. Well, if you're doing the Christian thing right now, I don't want any part of it."

Patrick turned again and hurried his step.

Nothing I say will make any sense, he told himself. *I don't even understand myself.*

"Go ahead and run, Patrick," Jefferson yelled at him. "You're becoming very good at it."

Patrick tried not to listen as he stumbled away. He took a different way through the town, past a row of neglected storefronts he usually stayed away from. No one followed him. He didn't bother to step around the mud puddles. And he didn't even look up when he heard a group of men laughing.

"Look here, boys, it's the darkie lover! Must be lost to be in this part of town."

Patrick wiped his face on his sleeve and looked up out of the corner of his eyes. He didn't dare turn his head when Sebastian Weatherby laughed.

"Darkie lover," repeated Sebastian, and he laughed again. Patrick tried to hurry by, but a few of the men stepped into the street to surround Patrick.

"I am not!" Patrick backed up. It was the first thing that popped out of his mouth, and instantly he felt ashamed. But he couldn't take it back. And when he turned around, a couple of Sebastian's older friends were right there, waiting for him with their arms crossed. One had a black tattoo of a boxing kangaroo on his fore-arm, and the fellow's unfriendly grin revealed his top front tooth was missing.

That's probably what they're going to do to me, Patrick worried, and his hand went to his mouth.

Sebastian strutted over to the ring of men, then leaned into Patrick's face with a sneer.

CHAPTER 15

MYSTERY IN THE STABLE

"Well, now, you could have fooled me," said Sebastian. "Spending all that time over there at Dingo Creek. Then there's your mate, there . . . Luke, is it?"

This time Patrick held his tongue.

"What should we do with 'im?" asked the fellow with the missing tooth.

Sebastian crossed his arms and studied Patrick's face, then chuckled and stepped aside.

"Ah, go on." He waved his hand. "Go on home to your mum."

Patrick didn't wait for Sebastian or his friends to say anything else. He just put his head down and ran toward home. He didn't stop until he was safe in his bed, hiding under the covers.

"Patrick?" asked Michael, sitting on his cot. "Why are you in bed already? Are you sick?"

"Just tired, that's all." Patrick didn't move, didn't say anything else. Finally Michael gave up and got ready for bed himself.

With so many people sleeping in one small cabin, Mr. McWaid had figured out a way to make their own "rooms." Michael and Patrick each slept on raised cots in the far back corner of the cabin; Jefferson had been given a comfortable pad made of old blankets that rolled away each morning under Patrick's bed. A clothesline strung from front to back supported a white sheet like a kind of stage curtain. In the opposite corner Becky had her own "room," too. And Luke prefered to stay in his own lean-to outside.

"Are you sure you're not sick?" Michael tried again before climbing under his covers.

"I'm almost asleep, Michael. Please don't bother me."

But by the next morning Patrick didn't know how much he had actually slept or been awake. First Michael had woken him when he brought in his koala and began feeding him some leaves. Then Patrick thought he heard tools clattering out in the shed, but he decided it was probably a brush-tailed possum looking for a snack. He had seen them before around the cabin at night, cute little animals that reminded him of squirrels. Patrick's father started snoring from the front of the cabin as the rain fell even harder, and Jefferson rolled out of his bedroll and onto the bare wood floor with a grunt.

Patrick rolled over and tried to pretend for a moment that the day had already passed and it was nighttime again. Was it really morning?

Maybe if I keep my eyes closed, he told himself, *the cricket match will go away*.

But there was Jefferson, sitting on the floor next to Patrick's bed.

"Patrick, are you awake?"

"Uh-huh."

"Well, then, I need to tell you I'm sorry about what I said to you yesterday."

Patrick didn't know how to answer.

"Do you hear? I'm apologizing."

Patrick swallowed hard, still thinking.

"I was just trying to talk some sense into you, but I went and said some things that ought not to have been said."

The possum outside made a return visit, scratching at the shed door.

"And I don't blame you, Patrick, if you're still sore at me."

"I'm not angry," Patrick finally answered as he sat up straight. "But I still don't want to go to the game."

"What? Why not?"

Patrick sighed and looked around the room in the gray morning light. He lowered his voice.

"Look, Jeff, what happens if the Dingo Creek team loses? I don't think it's going to stop there. Sebastian's mean, and . . ." Patrick didn't want to go on, didn't want to even imagine what the bully might do.

"So all we have to do is win," smiled Jefferson.

Patrick shook his head. "It's not that simple."

His parents had slipped out of bed; Becky was up, too. Luke was still outside in his lean-to.

"We're all coming to see you and your friends play." Mrs. McWaid smiled over at them and began to rattle some pans around for breakfast. "The match starts at ten, does it not?"

"Ten o'clock sharp, ma'am," chirped Jefferson, sounding more awake than Patrick thought he had a right to. Patrick looked out the front door a moment and wished again for rain.

"Lots of rain," he whispered. "Then maybe the other team won't even show up." He didn't think anyone else heard him.

Three hours later Luke stood with his hands on his hips,

looking around the field where they would play, just north of Echuca.

"You got your wish," Luke told him, frowning and holding out his hand. "But we're still going to play. Even in this drizzle."

By nine-thirty a couple of people from town had come out to watch them set up the field. Jeff had already paced out the distance between the wickets, and he and Luke were setting out little rock boundaries every few feet, all the way around the oval playing field.

Moses and the others had arrived from Dingo Creek, as well, and even a few of the other aborigines had shown up to watch. Even Davey was there, whispering into his grandfather's ear, as usual. When he noticed Patrick his face lit up in a smile.

"Come over here, Patrick," Moses told him. Patrick shuffled slowly over.

"Yes?" Patrick kicked at the dirt with the toe of his shoe.

"I just wanted to thank you for standing with us," said the old man. The smile on his face was almost like his grandson's. "It means quite a bit to me."

"Standing?"

"Speaking well of my people. And your friend Luke. He always speaks well of you. He's told me about you."

Patrick nodded, and then he remembered to talk so the blind man could understand his answer.

"It's nothing," Patrick barely got the words out.

If only he knew what kind of a friend I really was, Patrick told himself as he slowly backed away. He could still hear himself shouting at Sebastian.

"I am not!" The words echoed in his mind.

Some of the aborigine boys were starting to practice with the ball out on the field. Patrick turned to see Sebastian and Will coming their way, bringing a parade of onlookers behind them, and he groaned softly.

"Mr. Dunsmuir at the Echuca Hotel paid for our playing clothes," crowed Sebastian, turning around for everyone to see his white trousers and matching long-sleeved shirt. "Very nice, wouldn't you say?"

Patrick had to admit the other team looked like a team.

"Is your team planning to show up?" asked Will, looking over the heads of the ragtag bunch of aborigines dressed in castoffs. Luke waved for the group to join him.

"Eight, nine, ten . . ." Sebastian counted their team with his finger. "Where's your eleventh player?"

Luke stood up a little straighter. "He's in jail, remember? We'll play with ten."

"If that's the way you want it."

Some of the other players in their matching white shirts and trousers began to laugh, and Patrick backed away from the playing field. He imagined it was going to be a long, embarrassing match.

Still, a few more people from town were gathering to watch; with about fifteen minutes to game time, twenty-five or thirty people had gathered. More were coming from town all the time. Becky was there, too, excitedly explaining something to Jefferson, moving her hands and pointing back toward town. Their parents stood watching, and even Mrs. Wilson was there, hanging back at the edge of the growing crowd. Patrick was relieved she had left her dog at home. He drifted back toward town, moving against the people coming their direction.

"Hey, Patrick!" called Jefferson. "Listen to what your sister just found out."

Patrick frowned and glanced quickly over at Will and Sebastian, who were paying them no attention.

"Come on, don't you want to hear who owns that stable we were in the other day?"

"Shh!" Patrick hurried over to them and put his finger to his lips. "Not so loudly."

Jefferson rolled his eyes. "Oh, come. Tell him, Becky."

"I don't think he wants to know." Becky crossed her arms.

Patrick sighed. "Who?" he finally asked her.

"Well, if you must know, it was Richard Wilson."

"Was?" Patrick couldn't remember exactly who Richard Wilson was.

"Mrs. Wilson's former husband. He died, remember? She told us herself."

"Oh right." Patrick nodded. "*Mister* Wilson. So why is that so important to know?"

Becky gave his ankle a prod with her toe. "Don't you see? The stolen bridles were kept in the Wilsons' old stable. Who would have a key?"

"You mean besides Mrs. Wilson?" The answer seemed obvious, but they still didn't have any proof, one way or the other. "Doesn't make any sense to lock an old stable like that anyway."

The crowd cheered as the town team lined up for introductions. Mr. Dunsmuir, the stocky proprietor of the Echuca Hotel, was waving his hand and bowing like a master of ceremonies.

"I don't think I want to see this," said Patrick as he turned to go.

"Patrick—" said his sister.

"I'll see you later." Patrick waved without turning around and headed upstream through the crowds. As he hurried away, Jefferson's voice rang in his head.

"Go ahead and run, Patrick. You're becoming very good at it."

Patrick hurried away, dodging the people coming at him. Other voices seemed to echo in his memory, too, as clearly as if they were right next to him.

"Thank you for standing with us," Moses had said.

To him that knoweth to do good, and doeth it not, to him it is sin. The words began to blur together.

Patrick hurried aimlessly through the streets of Echuca, running around blocks and through alleys. Past the wharf, where six paddle steamers were tied up. Past Mullarky's General Merchandise and the Bridge Hotel. Past stables and stores, and then he was standing in front of the stable Becky had showed them. This time he heard the noise of a horse inside.

What's that? He tried to peek in through a couple of boards, but it was too shadowy to see. He started to pull at the loose board to slip inside but heard a noise behind him.

"Who—?" he began, whirling around in a panic. But it was only Davey, staring up at him with his wide eyes and big smile.

"Did you follow me here?" Patrick made a brushing motion with his hands. "You ought to be back at the match with your grandfather. Go on."

But Davey shook his head no, then grabbed at Patrick's sleeve and tugged.

"Play," said the little aborigine boy. "You play. Come on, please?"

Patrick had to smile. "I can't play. I'm no aborigine. You go."

But Davey would not give up. He acted out the swinging motion of a cricket batsman, then made a clicking sound as if he had just hit the ball. Patrick had to smile, and for a moment he thought about what it would be like to play with the aborigines.

Maybe . . . he wondered to himself. *But what would Sebastian do?*

"Come on. Please?"

"I'm sorry. See you later." Patrick turned around and pulled back the loose board in the side of the stable and slipped inside.

Davey followed him in, and they both stood in the gloom for a moment.

"Looks like you're determined. Well, stay by me, then." Patrick gave up trying to shoo the boy away and stepped farther into the stable. He could hear an animal somewhere, and he stepped carefully through the dirty hay to a stall on the far end of the building. Two black, straight-backed horses chewed contentedly and stared curiously at the intruders.

Patrick ran his hand along the nearest animal's back. It looked dusty and dirty, as if it hadn't been brushed for a long time, and its mane was tangled and wild.

"Nice girl," cooed Patrick.

Davey slowly put up a hand to touch the animal, and when it stomped its foot he jumped.

"Gentle, see?" Patrick took Davey's hand and helped the younger boy stroke the horse. He felt a greasy patch on the horse's leg.

"What's this?" he asked himself, looking closer. He couldn't see much by the dim light that filtered in, but Patrick turned around and pointed at an old towel hanging on a nail.

"Hand me that towel, would you?"

Davey understood the sign language and returned with the towel. Patrick began to rub, and the horse shuffled away.

"Something is wrong here," Patrick told himself. "Very wrong."

CHAPTER 16

THE BIG MATCH

"Hold still, there, girl," Patrick told the horse. He spit on the towel and rubbed some more, and in a couple of minutes there was no mistaking a hand-sized blaze of white on the horse's shoulder.

"I don't know what kind of grease this animal was wearing," Patrick told his Davey, "but these are Mrs. Wilson's horses, I'm sure of it."

"Can't confuse my horses with any others," Mrs. Wilson had told them the first time they visited her house. Her horses were black as night—one with a spot of day on his shoulder, the other . . .

Patrick bent down carefully and rubbed on the other horse's ankles.

"Hold it!" mumbled Patrick. He removed just enough grease from the animal's legs to see what he was looking for.

Patrick stood. "Look at that. White ankles. These are Mrs. Wilson's horses, all right. Someone tried to cover it all up! Question is, who?"

Davey didn't look too impressed. He found the same can of black goo Jefferson had found the other day. But this time Patrick had a better idea what it was.

"Put that down," he told his friend, taking the flat tin and slipping it absently into his own back pocket. For a moment he thought of bringing the horses out of the stable, but then he realized whoever saw him would suspect *him* of being the thief.

No, that won't do, he told himself. *What do we do now?*

"Come play?" asked Davey, almost as if he had heard Patrick thinking.

Patrick looked at the two horses and thought for a moment, then he nodded. Winning the match seemed more important than ever now that the pieces to the horse-theft puzzle were starting to fall into place.

"Maybe, Davey. Let's go see."

Patrick and the little boy slipped out through the loose board and ran back to the playing field, with Davey squealing all the way. From the edge of the field, Luke was the first to notice them. It looked as if the game had already started, and one of the town players was hitting the ball at one end of the playing field. Sebastian, the other batsman, stood with his back to them.

"Are you still short one player?" asked Patrick, getting his breath back.

Luke raised his eyebrows. "Are you volunteering?"

Patrick looked down at Davey, then nodded yes.

"I was hoping you would change your mind," said Luke, smiling. "We'll show them what you can do."

"That's it, Patrick!" yelled Becky from the sidelines.

Patrick was almost afraid to look. Instead, he just slipped onto the field. Sebastian wheeled around.

"Wait a minute," he shouted. "You can't play."

"Why not?" asked Patrick. "Where is it written?"

"We agreed to play the aborigine team, is all." Sebastian wasn't backing down. "Not the aborigine team and a white boy. You can't play unless your face is as black as theirs."

Several people in the crowd murmured their support of Sebastian's argument. "It's only fair," said one.

"That's right," added another.

Jefferson trotted onto the field to help out. "He has a point, Luke," he whispered. "We're not going to win this argument."

Patrick bit his lip and put his hands on his hips, trying to think. The can in his pocket, though, gave him an idea. He looked over at the cluster of players from the town team, waiting their turn to bat.

"What did you say, Sebastian?"

Sebastian impatiently punched his fist into his palm. "I said, you can't play unless your face is as black as theirs. Now, get off the field and go watch like everyone else."

With a grin Patrick pulled out the can of black cream from his back pocket, opened it, and smeared a dollop onto his cheek.

"What are you doing?" asked Jefferson.

Patrick didn't answer. He stared straight at Sebastian as he smeared the goo all over his face. By the worn label on the side of the can, Patrick figured it was stage makeup, the kind white actors would put on their faces if they were playing the part of a black person.

In a moment Patrick's face was completely black. He smiled and looked around as the showers dried up and the sun peeked out from behind a cloud for the first time all morning. Everyone stared at him curiously and Will's mouth hung open. Even the Dingo Creek team looked at him as if he had gone crazy.

"You must be kidding," sputtered Sebastian, but he looked as pale as Will.

"No, just making a point." Patrick put his hands on his hips and stood as tall as he could in front of Sebastian. "I figured if you could paint your face black, I could, too."

The crowd was silent as people tried to make sense of what was going on.

"You're crazy. I don't know what you're talking about."

"I think you do." Patrick watched Sebastian's face closely to see if he was sweating. The accusation was a wild guess, he knew, but what if it was true? Maybe Mrs. Wilson was telling the truth about what she had seen the night her horses were stolen. Maybe she had seen a couple of black-faced young men across her meadow. Only maybe the black-faced young men weren't aborigines, but white men with black faces. . . .

Chewing on his lip, Sebastian hurried over and whispered to Will, the team captain. At first Will shook his head no, then they both turned back to Patrick and the aborigines. A couple of the Dingo Creek players had shuffled up to Patrick and grinned at the face paint. One of them put his finger to Patrick's cheek and chuckled.

"If you want to make a fool of yourself," said Will blankly, "go ahead. Your team needs all the help they can get. We'll just add one of our reserves. Eleven to eleven."

Patrick nodded as the umpire stepped forward. Several people in the crowd murmured their confusion.

"Now that you have the teams settled," announced Mr. August Foster, the news reporter from Melbourne who had agreed to umpire the match, "would the Echuca batsmen please take their places so we can get this match under way?"

Still looking at Patrick and chuckling, the Dingo Creek players found their positions on the field.

Patrick took his place at the "point" position, about fifteen paces away from where the Echuca batsmen would stand. He looked around at the growing crowd.

"Half the town, don't you think?" Patrick asked one of his teammates, a boy Moses called Bedgi-Bedgi. The boy may not have understood what Patrick said, but he nodded nervously.

And I know who they'll be cheering for.

Most of the onlookers still huddled under blankets or raincoats, though the drizzle had about dried up. Becky and Michael sat on wooden crates in front of their parents, who were surrounded by at least a hundred others, curious for a look at the aborigine team in action. Becky clasped her hands together in front of her in a kind of victory salute.

"You just watch what happens!" Patrick yelled her way. He held on to what he and Davey had seen in the stable, held it like a game plan.

Taking his turn to bowl, Luke stood at the far end of the long batting square, digging his toe nervously into the ground as he waited for Sebastian to take his place. Their wicket keeper had even found a pair of heavy leather work gloves for the occasion.

"Everyone ready?" yelled Luke. Serving as captain, he checked the team and directed them into position with hand motions. The aborigine boys hopped in place and nodded excitedly back at Luke from their spots scattered around the field. On the sidelines Jefferson paced in circles around Moses, stopping only to explain what was happening in the field.

Soon Sebastian strutted over to his wicket, smiling and nodding to the polite applause from the crowd. Checking over his shoulder, Will followed him to guard the opposite wicket, about seventy feet away, and leaned against his bat with a smirk on his face. His turn would come after Sebastian's.

"If one of them can hit it between the fielders," Patrick could hear his father explaining to Michael, "the two batsmen run back and forth, switching positions before the ball is thrown back. They get runs for that, or for hitting the ball out of the field. Four runs if it rolls across the outside line, six if it's hit in the air across the line. But the most important part is that the batsman can't let the bowler knock over his wicket with the ball or he's out."

Patrick grinned when he saw Michael's confused expression.

That's what I must have looked like, he thought, *the first time I heard Luke explain the rules*.

"Excuse me, boy." The umpire tapped him on the shoulder.

"Yes, sir?" Patrick stood up straight and turned around.

"That was a clever touch with the black face."

Patrick smiled and nodded, rubbed his forehead with his sleeve, and returned to his position.

"Play!" said the umpire.

Over and over Sebastian viciously swiped at every ball Luke bowled at him, sending it whistling far out into the field. While their teammates cheered from the sidelines, Sebastian and Will ran back and forth, hit after hit, run after run, and the score began to look lopsided.

"Doesn't matter how you bowl it at me," sneered Sebastian. "I'll just keep hitting it."

"Our team's job in the field is to catch the ball if it's hit in the air," Patrick heard his father patiently explaining the game to Michael. "Or they throw it back to their wicket keeper as quickly as they can if it was hit on the ground."

"How do we get rid of the batsman who keeps hitting it?" asked Michael.

Good question, thought Patrick, waiting for the next ball to come his way.

"If they can just throw it hard enough and the batsmen haven't returned to their places yet, their keeper can knock over the wicket to put one of them out."

By that time Sebastian was trotting back and forth between the two wickets after what must have been the twenty-fifth run. He waved at the crowd again and grinned at the players.

Patrick frowned. *Looks as if he's ready for us to come pat him on the back.*

Sebastian slowed to a casual trot, not even bothering to run back to his wicket, the place where he batted.

"I don't know what you're trying to prove with that black-face act," he growled quietly at Patrick.

Out of the corner of his eye, Patrick could see a fielder returning the ball with a wild swing of his arm. The ball came whistling through the air like a spear aimed at a rabbit in the bush, and it hit the wicket squarely. Sebastian froze in surprise only two steps from the safety of his crease—where he had hit the ball—and Patrick clapped to see the older boy caught off guard.

"Sorry, bad luck," Patrick told him as he picked up the ball with a grin. "You've been run out."

Sebastian lifted his eyebrows in surprise, then swiftly swung his bat with one hand to swipe the side of Patrick's knee.

"Ow!" Patrick yelled out and fell to the ground.

Sebastian was at his side in an instant. "Oh, I'm so sorry," he said, loudly enough for everyone to hear. "I didn't mean to hurt you."

The piercing look in Sebastian's eyes told quite another story, but Patrick could only clutch his knee in pain.

"Are you all right?" asked Luke, running up to see what had happened. Mr. McWaid and the umpire were there in a moment, as well.

"My knee," groaned Patrick.

"Oh, I feel so terrible for bruising you," repeated Sebastian. "I'm so clumsy."

"Can you walk, lad?" asked Mr. Foster, rubbing the throbbing knee. "I . . . I didn't see what happened."

Patrick struggled to his feet, but the pain nearly buckled his legs from beneath him. Still, he was determined not to limp, not with Sebastian watching.

"It was nothing," replied Patrick. "Just an accident."

"Yes, well, in any case, the batsman is out." The umpire signaled with one finger, but the match was far from over. The rest of the Echuca batsmen took their time, battering Luke and their other bowler for more and more runs. Patrick tried not to show the pain, but his knee throbbed whenever he put any weight on it. He avoided Sebastian's look whenever he could.

Thankfully, none of the other Echuca boys seemed to go on for as long as Sebastian had, not even Will, who was only mediocre with the bat. The incredible throwing arms and a few diving leaps from the aborigine fielders kept the match from stretching any longer.

"Well done," commented Mr. McWaid after one of their players had robbed the sixth or seventh Echuca batsman of a long hit. Still, by the time the last player on the town team was finally out, the Dingo Creek Eleven could barely drag themselves in from the field for the tea break. The score seemed uncountable, it was so high.

"Moses, tell them no long faces." Patrick tried to cheer them up. "We still have a chance."

Luke gave him a grim look, and Patrick could guess what his friend was thinking.

A chance to match their 115 runs?

After the break the first Dingo Creek batsman was a boy they called Ned, grinning and hopeful.

"Johnson and Richards, you're in the slips," announced Sebastian, pointing to his teammates and showing them what positions on the field they would play. "Masters, you play point, and Chamberlain, you're mid-off."

Finally the town team was arranged to Sebastian's satisfaction around the field, and he glared at the aborigine batsman.

"Don't let him knock the sticks over, Ned!" shouted Jefferson.

"I mean," Jefferson corrected himself quietly, "Don't let him bowl you. Or don't let him hit the sticks, or whatever they're called."

Patrick had to smile. *After all our practices, he still doesn't know the right words to use.*

Sebastian seemed to pay no attention and charged a few steps toward the Dingo Creek batsman. When he reached the point beside one of the wickets, he twirled his arm as if he were mixing a can of paint and released the red leather ball underarm-style.

The boy from Dingo Creek swung his bat desperately, but the ball had already bounced on the ground in front of him and nearly squirted past the wicket keeper.

"Did you see that one?" whistled Jefferson from the crowd. "It was a blur."

Patrick could only stare as Sebastian wound up once more, charged, and released another underarm ball that flew even more quickly than the first, crashing straight into the wicket. Some boys on the town team clapped as Ned turned and stared at the fallen sticks. It was his job as a batsman to protect the wicket.

"Only two balls!" cried Sebastian. "This is going to be a quick match."

"He didn't even have a chance to run," said Luke quietly.

"I think I like American baseball better," said Jefferson. "At least we get three strikes."

"This is not going to be pretty," decided Patrick as he paced the side of the field. He knew it was supposed to be a shortened match, not a day-long affair like some cricket matches he had heard of. But it wasn't supposed to be quite *this* short.

"Well played. But who's next?" Will grinned as he straightened out the wicket for the next batsman. As the wicket keeper, he was even wearing proper leg guards over his light-colored trousers.

The next Dingo Creek batsman quietly took up his spot between the two white chalk lines they called "creases" and stared at Sebastian, the bowler, just twenty-two yards away.

"Knock it for a six!" cheered Jefferson. But the boy could only graze the ball, and they watched helplessly as it popped up weakly into the air just over his head. A moment later the ball slapped into the grinning wicket-keeper's gloves.

"You're out," crowed Will.

"Not to worry." Luke trotted up to take the bat. "Could happen to anyone. We still have eight batsmen left."

His head down, the boy limped back to the sidelines. But the match wasn't over yet.

CHAPTER 17

DESPERATION PLAY

The next Dingo Creek batsman managed half a dozen runs, and the one after that, ten more. And when it was Sebastian's turn to bowl, several balls went so wide that the Dingo Creek team was awarded penalty runs. They all cheered when Luke, the ninth batsman, finally brought run number 100 with a long, whistling drive over the boundary.

"Home run!" shouted Jefferson, jumping up and waving his fists. This time Jeff didn't seem to mind when everyone stared at him. Will straightened out from his spot as wicket keeper behind the batsman, held up his hand, and walked up to Sebastian.

"What are they fussing about?" Jefferson wondered aloud.

Becky noticed a small figure pushing through the crowd.

"I don't know," she answered, "but look who's coming our way."

Patrick turned around to stare at Ruth Wilson. The woman's jaw was set as she stepped toward them, as if she were on a mission.

"Maybe she's here to shout at us again," Becky said as Mrs. Wilson stepped closer.

"Mrs. Wilson," said their father in his polite tone. "Good to see you here."

"G'day to you all." Ruth Wilson stood next to Becky, staring straight ahead without smiling. She didn't wait for an introduction.

"Looks like you've had your face in the fireplace, lad." Mrs. Wilson didn't look at Patrick when she said it.

"What?" Patrick touched his cheek and remembered. "Oh yes, right."

He didn't try to explain as they watched the match. A few minutes later Moses left the field with his grandson dragging him toward town. Luke was still the batsman.

"Where's he going?" asked Jefferson.

"Maybe he's hungry," suggested Patrick. His own stomach was growling.

"Do you know cricket?" Becky finally asked Mrs. Wilson, who hadn't moved from her spot next to them. "Our friend Luke is batting, and we're behind by just fifteen runs."

The woman narrowed her eyes and looked out at the field. "Never saw much purpose in sports or games."

Sebastian and Will changed places. As the new bowler, Will took a few warmup throws.

"Then you've come to watch your nephew?" Becky tried once more to be friendly.

At least she can't shout at us out here in public, thought Patrick, though Mrs. Wilson looked as if she had just bitten into a lemon. The older woman didn't answer, and then the audience gasped.

"He's been hit!" cried Mr. McWaid, jumping out into the field.

"What?" Patrick turned to look and saw Luke crumpled on the ground.

"Luke!" Patrick and Jefferson shouted at the same time. The two sprinted after Mr. McWaid.

"It was an accident." Will looked almost pleased with himself. Patrick noticed Sebastian walk up to the other boy and quickly shake his hand, making no effort to hide his grin. Mrs. Wilson noticed, too—she was staring straight at her nephew with a look that would have frozen boiling water.

"Someone get Dr. Thompson!" commanded Mr. McWaid.

Patrick kneeled at his friend's side. "Luke, where were you hit?" The growing goose egg on the side of Luke's head was answer enough. Patrick and his father rolled Luke over on his back, then tried to get him to sit up, but he seemed only half-awake.

"I think you're through for today," suggested Mr. McWaid.

"No!" Luke forced his dark eyes open. "We have to finish."

Patrick glanced back at Sebastian and Will, and Will quickly covered a grin with his hand.

"We're so sorry," said Will. Patrick knew he wasn't.

Patrick and Jeff each put one of Luke's arms around their shoulders, and they carried him off to the sidelines. Mrs. McWaid tried to help him feel better with a damp handkerchief placed on his bump, but nothing seemed to do any good. Mrs. Wilson pushed her way to Luke's side.

"Are you all right?" she asked, crouching down next to him. Carefully she touched a finger to his head, and Patrick guessed it was the first time in her life she had been so close to an aborigine.

"Yes, ma'am," he answered quietly. "I'm fine."

But Luke swayed on the box where he sat.

"No, you're not," she snapped back. "I've done some nursing in my day. You were hit right in the temple with that dreadfully hard ball, and you have the nerve to tell me you're all right? You most certainly are *not* all right."

Is this the same old woman who chased us away from her house? Patrick wondered.

"It glanced off to the side." Luke closed his eyes. "An accident . . ."

"Foolishness," she replied. "That ball was thrown directly at you, and on purpose. I may be a silly old woman, but I'm not ignorant. Not anymore."

She stood up and glared at her nephew.

"Shall we finish the match?" Will asked from a distance.

Luke offered Patrick his bat. "It's Patrick's turn."

Patrick took a deep breath and walked slowly onto the field with the bat. Sebastian would be bowling now, and he faced Patrick with a scowl that sent shivers down his spine.

"Go ahead," Patrick whispered, rubbing his hands on the legs of his pants and digging his feet in. He tried to ignore the pain in his knee. "Bowl it as hard as you can."

Patrick didn't move from his crouched position, his bat almost touching the ground. Every muscle felt wound up like a spring, ready to smite the first ball that came near him.

After his staring act was done, Sebastian finally began his approach, six steps, then a high skip and a stirring-motion delivery. The red blur of a ball whistled through the air at Patrick, hit the ground once in front of his feet, and hardly bounced at all.

But Patrick uncoiled from his crouch, took a half step forward, snapped his wrists, and sent the ball sailing straight over Sebastian's head and between two fielders.

"That's it!" shouted Jefferson while Patrick hustled to trade places with the other batsman on his team.

"Go, Patrick!" Luke urged him from the sidelines. For a moment it sounded to Patrick as if he had been learning American cheers from Jefferson.

Patrick went, hitting ball after ball, almost as well as Sebastian had. In fact, Sebastian started to stamp his foot down every time Patrick connected with a solid crack of the bat.

Town Team 115, Dingo Creek 112.

"Beginner's luck," Sebastian spat at him as he wound up and delivered once more, a wickedly curving ball that grazed the wicket but didn't knock anything over.

That was close. Patrick breathed a sigh of relief and took an extra-long step toward the bowler.

The crowd "oohed" when the ball came flying past Patrick's ear and the wicket keeper somehow kept the ball in play.

Only three runs to tie, four to win.

The next bowl was low and wobbly, but Patrick had a good eye for where it was headed. He swung hard and the ball glanced off the side of the bat before dribbling away to the side. No runs scored. Again the crowd took a deep breath.

Concentrate, Patrick told himself.

The next bowl was slower, but it spun terribly. Patrick took advantage of the change, sending it looping over Will's head.

"Run!" hollered Patrick as he quickly changed places with the other batsman, ignoring the nagging pain in his leg. That would be a single; he touched the ground with his bat before he looked over his shoulder to see if they could stretch the hit into two runs. He felt a foot under him, and the next moment he was on his back, looking up into Will's smirk.

"Wait a minute!" he cried. The umpire was following the ball and hadn't seen Will trip Patrick.

"So sorry," sneered Will, backing away. "You'll have to be more careful where you step."

"Foul!" yelled Jefferson from the sidelines. "Patrick was tripped!"

Patrick started to complain to the umpire, but for the moment Mr. Foster was only watching the ball and waving to the crowd. Patrick picked himself up and stared silently at Will. The sneaky move had obviously cost the Dingo Creek team a run. Will caught the ball and stood there, challenging Patrick to speak.

"Nice umpire, eh?" said Will.

Patrick didn't answer. *Only two more*, he thought, and he concentrated on batting again. Several hours of play had passed now, and he was breathing hard.

Patrick nodded to his teammate Bedgi-Bedgi, who was set to run. Around the field the other team was crouching, ready to catch him and win the match. And out of the corner of his eye, Patrick noticed two horses approaching the field from the outskirts of town.

Mrs. Wilson's horses? he thought. Another quick glance told him it was true. Moses sat atop one, while Davey led both black horses their way. Davey waved as Sebastian wound up.

Wait until Will sees, Patrick thought as he connected with a *smack* and the ball sailed over their heads. One run at least; perhaps two. Bedgi-Bedgi grinned and sprinted while Patrick tried to keep up with him.

"Again!" Patrick touched his bat to the ground and turned

around for the return trip for another run. It would be close, he knew, but it was the tying run.

The fielder caught up to the ball just as Moses led the horses right onto the field.

Will stood dumbfounded, his hands at his sides, and the ball sailed right past him.

"One more!" yelled Patrick, and they galloped around for the winning run before Will finally moved.

"We'll bowl that last ball again," shouted Will. "There are animals on the field."

"Those aren't just any animals," said Mrs. Wilson, breaking away from the crowd and hurrying up to Moses. "These are my horses!"

In the craziness of the next few minutes, Patrick couldn't quite tell what was going to happen. His teammates were jumping up and down, clapping each other on the back.

"Yes, but how do we know these two aren't the thieves themselves?" objected Will. "They could have just brought them back to make it look as if someone else stole them."

"I'd believe you had I not seen what you did to that boy, Luke, today." A red-faced Mrs. Wilson shook her finger at her nephew. "All the lies you told me. No, I will not be made a fool any longer."

"But, Aunt Ruth, you don't understand—"

"Oh, I do indeed, for the very first time. Those two thieves I saw—that was you and your friend Sebastian with black painted faces, was it not?"

Will's face clouded. "No, of course it wasn't."

"Don't you lie to me again, young man."

"I would never lie to you, Aunt Ruth."

But even Patrick could see that Will was now sweating. Will bit his lip nervously, trying to avoid his aunt's stare. Finally he took a deep breath and looked at his feet.

"All right. We were going to give the horses back, Aunt Ruth, honestly we were. But . . ."

Mrs. Wilson stood her ground as Will wiped his brow with the back of his hand.

"But, you see, we were simply borrowing them for a while. No harm done. After this was all over, we were going to quit. . . ."

"You have *that* part correct, at least."

"The match is over," announced Mr. Foster, and no one dared question him as the aborigines cheered. "Dingo Creek is the winner."

"Sebastian!" yelled Will as the crowd closed around them. "I told you to hide the horses somewhere else! If you'd kept up your end of the . . . Sebastian?"

But while Sebastian had slipped away, it was clear Will wasn't going anywhere. Constable Fitzgerald stepped in to take charge.

Becky walked over to Patrick and messed his hair. "Good job, little brother," she told him with a smile.

"What about Luke?" worried Patrick.

Luke was still unsteady on his feet, but he tried to stand as the doctor came hurrying out from town.

"I heard one of our boys was down." He scanned the crowd. The remaining town team players stood around the edge of the crowd, looking confused.

"Over here!" said Mrs. McWaid, holding on to Luke's arm. "This young man was hit in the head by a ball."

"Oh." The doctor paused and caught his breath, his mouth open for a moment. "I thought—"

"What did you think?" Patrick's mother gave the doctor no room to back away as she stood to face him. "You thought it was one of our town boys? And were you going to take care of this one?"

"Mrs. McWaid," stuttered the doctor, "I think it's going to be well enough."

"Of course it's going to be well enough, because you're going to aid this young man." Mrs. McWaid handed Patrick a handkerchief. "Here, Patrick, run down to the river for me, will you, and rinse this out? Hurry along."

Patrick did as he was told, running down a narrow trail through the bushes to the edge of the Murray. The water felt cold but good, and he splashed his own face with water before turning around to run back with the wet handkerchief—but it wasn't going to be that easy. Sebastian Weatherby blocked his way, his eyes blazing like a wild animal's.

CHAPTER 18

SPECIAL EDITION

"Everyone knows about you now, Sebastian." Patrick gathered up all his courage. "Mrs. Wilson—"

"Doesn't matter anymore." Sebastian's face was blotchy and red, and he was still breathing hard. If Patrick hadn't known better, he might have guessed that the older boy had been crying. "It's all over."

"*What's* all over?" asked Patrick, moving toward the river. "Your lies about the aborigines?"

Sebastian moved to block Patrick's way, then grabbed Patrick by the front of the shirt.

"You and your sister. I warned you."

Patrick tried to pull himself free but only suceeded in tumbling them both into the ankle-deep water. Sebastian wrestled him to his knees in the mud.

"Let go of me!" Patrick tried to squirm free, but it was no use. "What did I ever do to you?"

"Everything was fine around here until you and your sister got in the way." Sebastian practically sobbed the words. "And now it's all because of you that I have to leave town—"

"You had the nerve to blame me for stealing those horses."

When Sebastian shifted his weight, Patrick took the chance to twist all the way around. He put his hands up and tried to get away, but Sebastian was just too big for him.

"When my father prints it all in the newspaper," said Patrick, "they'll find you and—"

Sebastian roared like a bull and held Patrick's head under the water until he was fighting for breath.

He's going to drown me right here! Patrick panicked as he struggled to lift his head.

"Your father's not going to print a word of this!" screamed Sebastian.

"Yes, he is," gasped Patrick. He struggled and squirmed, not sure how far Sebastian would go with his threats. Finally Sebastian eased his grip and looked up at a noise in the bushes. In a second he was on his feet, leaving Patrick on his back in the mud.

"Patrick!" yelled a man, crashing through the bush toward them. Sebastian pointed a warning finger at Patrick.

"This is not over," he wheezed. Patrick was sure this time there were bitter tears in the boy's eyes.

"Patrick, are you down there?" came the man's voice once more. It sounded like Mr. Foster, the newspaper reporter.

"If you say anything, I'll find you." Sebastian pointed his finger at Patrick's face, then sniffled.

I'm sure you will, thought Patrick. Sebastian disappeared along the bank of the Murray just before Mr. Foster came stumbling through the bush. Patrick barely had enough time to stand up and catch his breath.

"Oh, there you are," said the newspaper reporter, straightening up. He looked at Patrick with surprise. "The constable took that fellow Will in for questioning, and your family went back up to town with your friend Luke. They were wondering about you. I have to get back there."

"Is he walking?" Patrick tried to look casual, as if he always took baths in cold, muddy rivers with all his clothes on.

"Oh sure. But your mother had to shame the doctor into taking a look at him. Quite a scene. Glad I made it. What about you, though? You look terrible. . . ." His voice trailed off with the words, and he gazed up and down the quiet river. There were no riverboats in sight, no birds, nothing. Only the quiet, sure-flowing brown Murray. "What was all the noise I heard down here?"

Patrick lowered his head and squeezed his hands into fists. "I think I need to see my pa. We're going to need some more help, fast."

Without another word Patrick hurried toward town.

"But what on earth happened back there?" asked Mr. Foster, running to keep up with Patrick.

"I'm sorry." Patrick tried to save his breath. "I'd better tell my father first."

He paused for a moment at the outskirts of the city, looking up High Street.

"He said he was going back to his office." Mr. Foster put his hands on his knees and wheezed. "But hold on. I'm not used to running like this. You fellows gave me a bit of exercise in that cricket game. I hope I managed all right."

Patrick wasn't listening. He took the fastest way to the newspaper office, back through the alley and around to the front door. The door was locked, but the inside of the *Riverine Herald*'s office was full of people.

"Patrick!" His little brother came and unlocked the door. "Where have you been? We're all in here, and Mr. Foster went out to fetch—"

Mr. Foster came around the corner, still gasping for breath, and stumbled though the door behind Patrick.

Inside, Mr. McWaid was ordering people in all directions. Becky sat at a table piled high with papers, writing as he dictated. Mrs. Wilson was there, too, her face flushed with excitement. Their mother was laying out food on another table while Michael scurried around the group.

"Looks like a party," said Patrick, hurrying up to his father.

"Thanks for finding him." Mr. McWaid pointed at Mr. Foster. "Patrick, where have you been?"

"I went to the river the way Ma asked, Pa. But Sebastian . . ." He hesitated when he saw Mrs. Wilson. She waved a hand at him.

"It's fine, child, you can say it. My nephew is going to have to take responsibility for what he's done. So is that horrible Sebastian Weatherby."

Patrick looked from his father to Becky and Mrs. Wilson.

"Mrs. Wilson is helping us put together a special story, Patrick, on the horse thefts and the cover-up. She knows all about who *really* did it."

"And how they tried to make it look as if the aborigines did it," put in Becky, not looking up from her paper. "And then us."

"You saw Sebastian?" Mr. McWaid looked concerned.

Patrick sighed and wiped the last of his face paint off with a handkerchief. "He wasn't too happy."

"Foster, you'd better go tell the constable about this," said their father. "Not that I expect him to move more quickly than he has."

Patrick bit his lip, remembering Sebastian's wild promise.

"Your father's not going to print a word of this!"

"Well, make yourself useful," interrupted Mrs. McWaid, pouring milk from a pitcher. "It looks as if we're staying here tonight to help your father."

"Pa's boss said we could use the apartment upstairs if we need it." Michael looked excited, as if it were a great adventure to sleep in town instead of at the cabin or on the paddle steamer.

Patrick smiled, too. "That's great!" he said. "But what do I do?"

"Your sister is writing the story with Mrs. Wilson's help," Mr. McWaid said, pacing the floor. "But there's no one here to help us set and print. And this is too big of a story to wait. You're going to get ink on your hands tonight."

Mr. Foster ran out the door, scribbling furiously on his notepad. "This turned out to be more of a story than just the aborigine cricket team, didn't it? Wait until it runs in Melbourne!"

Hours later Patrick looked down at his ink-smudged fingers as he worked the big crank on the printing press back and forth the way his father and Mr. Foster had shown him. His arms ached, but it was almost fun.

"Special Edition!" screamed one of the headlines Becky had set by carefully lining up trays full of lead type. It had taken longer than they hoped, especially after Michael accidentally knocked over several trays of letters that had already been laid out.

But there it was, finally, and Patrick slowly read the story Mrs. Wilson had told them. He managed one line with each sheet he peeled from the printing press. First the odd-looking horse thieves who wore English clothes, the ones she could hardly see. Her nephew Will had convinced her it had been aborigines, even though she had known there was something strange about them. She said she had been confused by the dark faces, taken in by her persuasive nephew. He was, after all, the one who had supported her ever since her husband had died.

Then had come the threats from Sebastian, and the time she had seen him talking with a stranger outside her property in the middle of the night. Probably the same stranger Patrick had seen talking with Sebastian the night of the corroboree. She had even overheard them talking about which horses they would grab next. Becky explained how she had found out about Mr. Wilson owning the old stable, while Patrick shared the discovery of the horses. And there it was, every word in print, with "By Rebecca Elisabeth McWaid" right at the top.

"Truth Uncovered About Echuca's Horse Thefts!" read one of Becky's smaller headlines, and then, "Aborigines Falsely Accused to Divert Attention, Says Eyewitness."

"It's all there, isn't it?" Patrick's father said, taking a turn at the press. "Did we leave out anything?"

Patrick smiled and shook his head, wiping his hands with an ink-black rag. "I just wish we knew where Sebastian was. I feel sorry for him."

Mr. McWaid nodded his head. "At least that Will character is telling the world all that he knows. Hard to believe those two were actually part of a ring to steal horses all over the state. And then trying to make everyone else look guilty instead of themselves."

Patrick tried not to rub his eyes as his father pulled the last sheets from the printing press several hours later. The wall clock ticked and he could hear Mr. Foster snoring.

One o'clock in the morning.

Mr. McWaid blew at the wet ink on the page and smiled at his son.

"That's about all we can do for today, son. Why don't you go upstairs and get some sleep? I'm going up that way myself."

Patrick's father blew out the kerosene lantern on the table, and they tiptoed between the piles of freshly-printed papers and the printing press to the stairway that led upstairs. Patrick paused for a moment, listening to Mr. Foster's snoring, and once more heard Sebastian's words echoing in his ears.

"Your father's not going to print a word of this!"

"Oh yes, he is," Patrick said to the darkness. "We just did."

"What did you say, Patrick?" his father whispered from the top of the stairs.

"I said we did it, didn't we, Pa?"

Mr. McWaid chuckled in the darkness. "Come on up and get some sleep."

Patrick had to smile when he thought about what they had done. Standing up to the horse thieves. Becky and her news article. The cricket match. As far as the voice that told him to run away, back to what he once knew in Ireland . . . well, he couldn't seem to hear it anymore.

"Pa?"

"Yes, son?"

"We're not going to move back to Ireland, are we?"

"What makes you think of that, now?"

"I'm not sure. But I don't want to go back anymore."

Mr. McWaid paused for a moment before finally answering. "No one else wants to go back, either."

Patrick made his way to the cot his mother had laid out for him and crawled under the blanket. But even though his body was exhausted, sleep was the last thing Patrick had on his mind. Pictures of the day flashed before him as he lay on his blanket. Mostly scenes from the cricket match, Luke's big smiles when he hit the ball, or the cheer of the crowd when they won. He tried not to think of Sebastian and Will, but he saw them, too. He remembered the feeling of panic when Sebastian dunked his head underwater. And he remembered again the poisonous words: *"Your father's not going to print a word of this!"*

"Stop saying that!" he whispered to himself as he sat up. No one else stirred in the apartment, but Patrick heard a sound that sent a shiver up the back of his neck.

At first the noise was soft, almost like a tree branch rubbing against the back door in the wind. But there were no trees in the alley. It was the sound of a doorknob downstairs, a tiny squeak.

Someone was coming in the back door!

CHAPTER 19

BUCKET BRIGADE

Patrick slipped out from under his toasty blanket and padded across the cold, bare wooden floor in his stocking feet, then carefully slipped down the stairs. He felt his way with his toes.

Who would try to sneak in here tonight? he wondered. And there it was again, the squeak and rattle of the back door.

By the time Patrick was down the stairs, he heard another squeaking noise.

"Patrick, is that you?" Michael's soft whisper came floating down the stairs.

"Go back to bed." Patrick waved him off, even though it was too dark to see. The only light came from outside as a man with a lantern ran past shouting.

"What's that?" This time Michael didn't whisper as he hurried down the stairs to stand next to Patrick. Another lantern flew by, then another.

"Something *is* going on out there," Patrick agreed, and they stared out the newspaper office's front window to get a better look.

"Michael?" They heard their mother's sleepy voice from upstairs. "Michael, are you down there? What's that noise?"

"People are running around out on the street!" Michael called back.

Mr. Foster didn't seem to hear any of it; Patrick imagined he was still sleeping in the corner. A moment later Becky and their father had joined them at the window.

"Everyone's carrying buckets," said Becky. "There's a fire!"

It didn't take them long to pull on their clothes, and a minute later Patrick, Becky, Michael, and their father were out the door to follow the firemen. Windows flew open up and down the street as people poked their sleepy heads out into the damp night.

"Whose place is burning?" a woman asked, but they could only follow the crowd down Hopwood Street toward the edge of town and the orange glow in the sky.

"Pa, do you know where that is?" asked Becky. After a couple of blocks of limping along behind his sister, Patrick thought he knew too.

"It's Mrs. Wilson's place!" shouted Patrick, and by that time he could hardly hear himself over the roar of the men running with their buckets. His knee still ached.

"Stay close to me," commanded their father, and they found a place on the edge of Mrs. Wilson's fence to watch the flames leap higher and higher into the night sky. Some of the men had formed a line of buckets from a horse-watering trough next door, but they needed more help.

"Come on!" said Luke as he flew by and slapped Patrick on the shoulder. Jefferson was right behind him.

"Luke, what are you doing up?" asked Patrick, joining in the frantic bucket brigade. With more help, they didn't have to run back and forth to pass the buckets, and the buckets came faster and faster. "You're supposed to be in bed."

"I told the doctor I was fine. And Jeff was just making a nuisance of himself, sleeping on the floor in the clinic."

"Hurry up!" shouted Constable Fitzgerald from the head of the line. He wore dark pants, and his suspenders draped loosely over a white undershirt. It was the first time Patrick had ever seen him without his uniform.

Water splashed on their feet as Patrick passed the bucket to Becky, who passed it to Jefferson and on down the line. Just like that, they had joined a bucket brigade.

Faster, Patrick told himself as he passed along more and more buckets. He didn't dare look, but he could feel the flames growing hotter and hotter, even as his arms started to ache from the weight of the water-filled buckets.

"Faster," he whispered, but Luke straightened out and didn't take the next bucket Patrick tried to hand him. Patrick could guess why as he finally looked again at the flames and watched in horror as the cabin collapsed in a shower of sparks. All that was left was the old, fallen fence around the pasture and the stone angel in Mrs. Wilson's front yard. Even the thick vines that had nearly hidden the statue had been cooked off.

"Forget the house!" yelled the constable, and they stood there with their buckets, staring in silence at the awesome power of the flames.

"Do you see her?" wondered Becky, putting down her bucket. "Where's Mrs. Wilson?"

"There." Mr. McWaid pointed across to the other side of the yard, where they could see Mrs. Wilson crumpled against one of the volunteer firefighters, her shoulders heaving in the flickering lights. "I'll be right back."

Their father returned in a minute, his arm around Mrs. Wilson. She was still barefoot. Even though they could still feel the heat from the fire, she was shivering.

"Mrs. Wilson." Becky stepped up to comfort the woman. "We're here for you. Everything is going to be all right."

Mrs. Wilson's lips moved, but no sound came out. Her soot-smudged face was set with tears, and she looked fearfully back over her shoulder at the remains of her home.

"Hannibal," she finally whispered, and they all leaned in to hear what she was saying.

"What did you say, Mrs. Wilson?" asked their father.

"Hannibal," she repeated, coughing a little. "My Hannibal is still in there."

"Oh dear," gasped Becky. "I'm so sorry."

Their father looked at them for an explanation.

"Hannibal is her dog," Becky told him, and he nodded. Mrs.

Wilson stood there stiffly, tears running down her cheeks, shivering.

"I'm so sorry, Mrs. Wilson," said Luke, still holding his bucket. She looked at him as if she had never seen an aborigine in her life.

"You . . ." she managed to say through her chattering teeth. "Aren't you the young black fellow who was hit in the head?"

Luke nodded.

"Why did you come to help. . . ?"

She couldn't finish the question, and Luke stood there, dripping. At last he smiled weakly and shrugged his shoulders.

"You need to get back to the clinic, young man," said Mr. McWaid.

"I'll get you a coat, Mrs. Wilson," said Patrick, thinking of one he had seen hanging upstairs at the *Herald* office. Before anyone could say anything else, he turned and sprinted back down the road, happy to be away from the fire. Halfway there, he almost ran into his mother, who was walking their way with another woman from town.

"Ma, it was Mrs. Wilson's house."

His mother gasped when she heard the news.

"Burned to the ground. I'm going to get a coat for her now."

Patrick's mind raced as he ran back through town, now lit up like during a festival.

How would the fire have started? he wondered. *Could it have been set?* If it had been, he had a pretty good idea who would have done the setting.

He felt a draft when he pushed open the door of the *Riverine Herald*, as if the back door was open, too.

"Hello?" His voice seemed to echo in the empty building.

I'm just imagining things, he told himself when no one answered, and he started upstairs to find Mrs. Wilson a coat. Halfway there, he heard a squeak from the back door, then the sound of a heavy load being dragged along the floor.

Someone's in the back! he told himself, and this time he knew his ears weren't playing tricks on him.

Quietly he tiptoed back down the stairs and through the dark office. He caught his bare toe on the leg of a chair but bit his tongue to keep from crying out in pain.

Do I run for the constable? he wondered, still inching forward. The dark figure dragged a big bundle through the back door, mumbling the whole time. As Patrick tiptoed closer, he tripped over a pile of newspapers and lost his balance in the dark.

"Oh!" He couldn't help calling out as he tumbled through the door and onto the floor next to the printing press. On his back, he could see flames in the alley—and Constable Mitchell poised over the press, a sledgehammer over his head.

The sight made no sense. *Constable Mitchell?*

Before Patrick could get to his feet, the assistant constable stood over him, the hammer still poised as a threat above his shoulder.

"What are you doing here?" snarled the young man, planting a heavy boot on Patrick's stomach. His face was smudged with soot. "Everyone was supposed to be down at the fire."

Patrick could smell the smoke from burning newspapers just outside the door, and he heard a horse whinnying in fright. But with everyone from town watching Mrs. Wilson's burning house, no one would notice the bonfire in the alley.

"I came back to . . ." Patrick stuttered. "But you're—"

"I'm just evening the score a bit," interrupted the young man, spitting like a snake. He seemed a different man from the one Patrick had seen before. Horribly different. And Patrick had heard almost the exact same words just a few hours ago from Sebastian.

It all made sense now, in a chilling sort of way. "You're one of them!" said Patrick. "You're one of the horse thieves."

"One of them?" laughed Mitchell—a crazy, twisted laugh. "I tell them what to do."

This time Patrick wasn't surprised as he realized the mysterious voice he had heard talking to Sebastian the night of the corroboree had belonged to Mitchell. "And you probably even set the fire at Mrs. Wilson's house, didn't you, so no one would see you here. And no one would ever guess."

"That's enough, boy."

Patrick could hardly breathe with the weight of Mitchell's boot pressing harder and harder on his ribs. Any harder . . .

"No one was in danger before," said the man, looking around nervously. "I even waited until Will's aunt was out of her house. But now you're in the way, young fellow. This is different."

"You're horrible," shouted Patrick. "Horrible and—"

"I said, quiet!" Mitchell pointed at the printing press. "Another word, and I'll do the same to you as I'm going to do to this press."

"Don't—" gasped Patrick, but Mitchell's first swing sent sparks flying from the printing press as metal hit metal.

"You're going to wish you stayed in Ireland." Mitchell grunted and took another swing. "I was doing the town a favor by getting rid of those darkies. Nothing wrong in that, is there?"

By that time Mitchell was swinging wildly at the press, sending metal parts flying. One hit the floor next to Patrick's head, another struck Mitchell in the chest. Patrick covered his head while Mitchell laughed and kept swinging.

"But what are we going to do with *you*?" asked Mitchell.

Patrick squeezed his eyes shut, too scared even to pray. He peeked up to see the door to the front room squeak open again, framing Mr. Foster in the light.

"Stay where you are," ordered the newspaperman. He was holding not a weapon but his pen and reporter's notebook. "I've written down all you've just said for the *Melbourne Sunday Times*. Interesting story—Constable's Assistant Turns Horse Thief."

Mitchell hesitated for only a moment between the front and back doors. Mr. McWaid had appeared behind the news reporter, blocking the way out the front. And as Patrick rolled away to safety, he saw two other men in the alley framed by the burning bonfire of newspapers. One looked like Constable Fitzgerald.

"Mitchell!" boomed Constable Fitzgerald. "What kind of humbug is this?"

Like a cornered bear, Mitchell wasn't giving up easily. He took one look at the constable in the alley and tried to push through the door to the front office like a battering ram. His only obstacle was Patrick, who was still trying to get up.

"Patrick!" his father warned him. "Get out of the way!"

Patrick couldn't move quickly enough as Mitchell tumbled over him. For a moment Patrick was staring straight into Mitchell's snarling face, but it was almost as if the young man didn't see him. Then suddenly Patrick was pulled out of the pileup. It took three men to pin Mitchell to the floor.

"He set the fire at Mrs. Wilson's," explained Patrick breathlessly. "Did you hear? He admitted as much. He's behind all the horse stealing, too!"

"Are you mad, Mitchell?" Constable Fitzgerald grabbed his assistant by the collar, and the younger man melted like butter in a warm room. Someone else moved in the doorway to the front room.

"You!" cried Mrs. Wilson, her voice quivering in anger. Patrick realized she must have heard everything.

For a moment Patrick thought the woman might attack, but she stopped with one foot through the doorway when she heard a loud barking in the back of the shop, then another yell.

"Patrick!" Becky yelled from the back of the building. "Pa! Look what I found!"

Patrick wasn't quite sure if Becky had found a dog, or the dog had found Becky. But a huge animal dragged her through the office by a short rope, looking singed and burned and still as big and ugly as ever.

"Hannibal!" cried Mrs. Wilson, falling to her knees. "You're the first good news I've had all night."

The huge black-and-brown dog found his master, then covered her with licks from his hand-sized tongue. Without another word Constable Fitzgerald pulled his assistant out and down the street, while Mrs. Wilson buried her face in the dog's fur. When she finally looked up, her face was almost as black from soot as Patrick's had been for the cricket match.

"Just look at yourself, Mrs. Wilson." Becky began to giggle in the strangeness of the moment.

"Becky, stop that." Mrs. McWaid had stepped back into the office and put her hands on her daughter's shoulders. "You mustn't."

But then she caught sight of Mrs. Wilson's face and couldn't help herself.

Mr. McWaid caught the giggles from her, then Patrick and Mr. Foster. And when Mrs. Wilson saw her reflection in the window, she joined in, too. Hannibal howled at the odd bunch of humans he had run into, which only made them laugh more.

"Wait until I tell Jeff and Luke," said Patrick. "Constable Mitchell was the mastermind! He was really behind all this trouble."

"Who would have believed it?" His father shook his head. "But look at us. Our papers are burning in the alley, the press is a wreck, and Mrs. Wilson's house is a pile of ash. And here we are, laughing."

"We must be crazy," agreed Mrs. Wilson, wiping the tears from her sooty face. Then she turned to Becky and Patrick. "But I tell you, I owe everything to these two young ones." She patted Becky on the head. "Especially you, dear."

"Thank you." Becky bowed her head, suddenly looking very shy. "But . . ."

Patrick heard a noise back in the alley, but he was almost afraid to look.

"Hey there," shouted Mr. Foster, who had stepped out to the alley, "are you all going to stand around talking and leave me to do all the work?"

Patrick could see the man batting at the low flames with a broom. At that point there was more smoke than anything else.

"What a mess," he said, trotting back to join the newsman.

"Sure it's a mess, but only a few bundles on the top and sides really burned. Look, pull those off."

The reporter was right. Under the blackened sheets of a few burning bundles, Patrick removed untouched stacks of newspapers.

"How about that!" cheered Patrick.

"Don't burn yourself." Mr. Foster stomped out the last of the flames.

"Looks as if we still have enough to pass around town," said Becky, who had joined them to help. "And we may have a little help."

They looked around the dying bonfire to a small ring of dark, silent faces.

"We saw the fire in the sky," said the unmistakable voice of Moses as the old man stepped up to Patrick and Becky. He laughed. "Or I should say, some of the others saw it. I came along to find out if you needed help."

Patrick looked at his sister, who nodded, and Patrick squeezed the old man's outstretched hand. "You always know exactly what's happened, don't you?" Patrick whispered to the blind man.

Moses chuckled. "Don't need eyes to see when Patrick McWaid has done the right thing. The good thing."

The good thing, wondered Patrick. *Does Moses know that verse, too?*

"People will know the truth now. So we'll help you pass out your newspapers. And we'll get our people out of the jail."

"Thanks, Moses," Patrick managed to say as his throat tightened up. "I'm sorry I ran away at first. I'm sorry I didn't—"

"Ah yes." Moses put up his hand, smiled, and nodded. "What's important is that you make God happy now."

Moses looked more tired than ever, but he turned to the people around them and spoke to them in their language, soft and musiclike. Several of them laughed.

"What did you say?" asked Patrick.

"I said, 'Patrick McWaid isn't so bad, for a part-time aborigine.'"

Patrick wiped his cheek and laughed with the others.

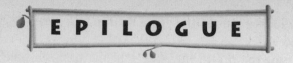
THE REAL CHALLENGE

Ever since Europeans first arrived in Australia in the 1700s, they haven't always gotten along with the original Australians—the people called "aborigines." Some of the English settlers felt that the dark-skinned people were just too different. Their language was different, and their customs were not like anything the English had known before.

European settlers also had very different ideas about how the land should be used and who should use it. For some, the aborigines were savages without souls who needed to be conquered. This attitude, of course, brought them into head-to-head conflict with the aborigines. Just like in North America, when settlers fought against the natives, the natives fought back. But in most cases, the settlers won. There were more of them, and they were armed with much more modern weapons than the aborigines.

To be sure, many of the settlers were fair-minded and wanted peace with native Australians. You can read from newspapers of the time how some people worked hard to convince everyone that the aborigines should be treated more fairly.

But real peace isn't easy. By the 1860s, when our story takes place, many of the aborigines had already died, disappeared, or been pushed farther inland—away from white settlements. Even today, the aborigine people struggle with who they are as a people.

So no one would say that history has been kind to the aborigines. But as Patrick and Becky would find out, by doing the right thing, they could make a difference—one person at a time.

Be sure to read Book 5 in the exciting
ADVENTURES DOWN UNDER!
Race to Wallaby Bay

When someone steals a small fortune from their grandfather, it's up to Patrick and Becky to get it back—or they'll have to sell the family paddle steamer! So the McWaids set off on a wild adventure down the Murray, searching for thieves in every port. A mysterious buyer for the *Lady Elisabeth* waits at the mouth of the river. And by the time Patrick learns a terrible secret that could change everything, he may be too late to make a difference.

Series for Middle Graders*
From Bethany House Publishers

ADVENTURES DOWN UNDER · by Robert Elmer
When Patrick McWaid's father is unjustly sent to Australia as a prisoner in 1867, the rest of the family follows, uncovering action-packed mystery along the way.

ADVENTURES OF THE NORTHWOODS · by Lois Walfrid Johnson
Kate O'Connell and her stepbrother Anders encounter mystery and adventure in northwest Wisconsin near the turn of the century.

AN AMERICAN ADVENTURE SERIES · by Lee Roddy
Hildy Corrigan and her family must overcome danger and hardship during the Great Depression as they search for a "forever home."

BLOODHOUNDS, INC. · by Bill Myers
Hilarious, hair-raising suspense follows brother-and-sister detectives Sean and Melissa Hunter in these madcap mysteries with a message.

JOURNEYS TO FAYRAH · by Bill Myers
Join Denise, Nathan, and Josh on amazing journeys as they discover the wonders and lessons of the mystical Kingdom of Fayrah.

MANDIE BOOKS · by Lois Gladys Leppard
With over four million sold, the turn-of-the-century adventures of Mandie and her many friends will keep readers eager for more.

THE RIVERBOAT ADVENTURES · by Lois Walfrid Johnson
Libby Norstad and her friend Caleb face the challenges and risks of working with the Underground Railroad during the mid–1800s.

TRAILBLAZER BOOKS · by Dave and Neta Jackson
Follow the exciting lives of real-life Christian heroes through the eyes of child characters as they share their faith and God's love with others around the world.

THE TWELVE CANDLES CLUB · by Elaine L. Schulte
When four twelve-year-old girls set up a business doing odd jobs and baby-sitting, they find themselves in the midst of wacky adventures and hilarious surprises.

THE YOUNG UNDERGROUND · by Robert Elmer
Peter and Elise Andersen's plots to protect their friends and themselves from Nazi soldiers in World War II Denmark guarantee fast-paced action and suspenseful reads.

*(ages 8–13)